Table of Contents

Accidental Soldiers

By

Ron L. Carter

RON L. CARTER

Copyright 2019 by Ron L. Carter

***

Published at Smashwords

* * *

Smashwords Edition, license notes

***

Disclaimer

The people and places appearing in this book, as well as the story, are fictitious. Any resemblance to real people, living or dead, is entirely coincidental.

***

***

4

Prelude

Searching for food was only possible under cover of darkness. Having been attacked by the Russian forces and their advanced weapons, no other option was feasible. The group was composed of four men and two women. They were all close friends and six college athletics who graduated from Cal Poly University in San Luis Obispo, California, ten years earlier. With only six people in their group, each had to pull their weight, and it was now Brian's turn. They were lucky not to have been discovered in their small hideaway tucked underneath the overpass. They were almost out of food and forced to take another risk.

In previous forages, they had narrowly escaped without casualties. It was a miracle, considering the technologically advanced arms the enemy soldiers were carrying and the vehicles they used. Whether it be their snowmobiles or their ATVs, it seemed nothing could get in their way. It was nearly impossible to dodge the precision of the deadly laser beams built into each vehicle, not to mention the accuracy of the AK-47s they carried strapped on their backs. Because of the odds against them, they knew they wouldn't be as lucky the next time they encountered the soldiers.

It was close to midnight, dark and quiet, and practically perfect conditions for Brian's trek. The conditions should have brought Brian comfort, but with the moon only occasionally appearing through the clouds, it made him feel lonely, and his travel felt ominous. He was the involuntary hunter of the group and one of the least experienced. He lived a somewhat sheltered life, raised on his family's dairy farm, which didn't leave him much time to join the boy scouts or learn skills like hunting or camping.

Being armed with a professional bow and arrows and a high-powered rifle with several rounds of ammunition would have been enough to protect himself in most situations. However, they would be of little help unless he were on constant guard. His mission took him past several deep crevasses and slippery terrain with steep slopes that could plunge him into an ice-cold river under the ice, and he could get swept away. Also, one wrong turn could land him in a sick game of hiding and seek with the enemy, where the soldiers were camped out just waiting for their next victim.

Brian had been on his quest for a few hours, and ever since he left, Cameron was restless and uneasy. From their college days together, he was close friends with Brian and was uncomfortable going out on this hunt alone.

He sat up, and the covers fell to his waist as he shivered from the brisk cold air and the thoughts driving him crazy. He was now kicking himself and wishing he had gone with Brian. He strained his ears for any distant sound. Not wanting to hear anything, he fought hard to let his mind drift back to better times when he was with his family. It worked only briefly as his thoughts gave into restlessness and fear. He finally got up from his warm sleeping spot and went to the opening of the hideout. He stood just outside the protected shelter area, straining his eyes and ears.

It wasn't long before Cameron heard the muffled short blast of an automatic weapon and two short bursts from what he also thought was a laser gun. His fear immediately swelled as he gritted his teeth and stiffened in anger. "Damn it, I knew it. I knew I should have gone with him." He now feared the worst might have happened to Brian.

Soon, all members gathered outside the hideout. They were looking wide-eyed and scared, and Cameron could hear the quivering in Staci's voice as she said, "Hey Cameron, what the hell was that? It sounded like the Russians were firing at something or someone.

I hope it wasn't Brian." Cameron grimaced, "I'm sure it was an automatic weapon and maybe some other type of weapon." He was familiar with the fear in Staci's voice. He'd heard that type of fear in the soldiers' voices under his command during his encounters with enemy soldiers in Afghanistan.

He knew Staci's fear was justified, "I don't know what happened, but I'm worried about Brian being alone. I think the soldiers may have gotten him."

They nervously talked to each other about what they'd heard and paced back and forth anxiously outside the hideout, hoping for Brian to return. As they waited, they talked about Brian possibly being killed or taken prisoner by the enemy soldiers.

Suddenly, they began to hear echoing, blood-curdling screams in the distance. It was such gut-wrenching sounds that it sent tingles up your spine as Rachel said, "Dear God, what are they doing to that poor guy."

Thomas moved close to Cameron and whispered, "Hey Cameron, that's Brian. They have him."

Cameron grabbed his rifle. "Yes, I know. Get your weapons, and we'll see what they do to him. Maybe we can get to him before they kill him. Let's keep our heads about us and move quietly and cautiously because we don't want to run into a trap."

The members quickly got their bows, arrows, and rifles as they followed in a line behind each other and slowly headed toward the tormenting sounds. As they made their way toward the screams, they carefully edged closer to the high-rise buildings and dense ice maze that was once the populated old town of Fresno. As they crept closer, Cameron whispered for everyone to keep an eye open for soldiers hiding in the buildings' higher levels. He wasn't sure if an ambush might be waiting for them around each dark corner, but he wanted everyone to be ready, just in case.

For a few minutes, it reminded him of one of the villages in Afghanistan where he and his soldiers were going door to door searching for the enemy when a force of well-armed insurgents attacked them, and three of his men got killed. Now, he was temporarily feeling back in that same situation. He had to shake the thought from his head as they dredged into enemy territory.

Everyone was becoming nervous as they got deeper and deeper into the downtown area and closer to the screams.

Once near the town center, Cameron stopped and quietly said, "I don't understand why Brian went so far into this area. We've never done that while we're out hunting for food."

Thomas whispered, "Yeah, we would've turned around way before we got this deep into the middle of town. It's just crazy."

Cameron gave the signal to continue toward the sounds slowly. As they got closer, the screams started to weaken. They had now softened into muffled painful moans and groans, almost like a whimper. They could see the light hanging from the middle of one of the abandoned intersection traffic signs. Cameron told the group to be careful not to give away their position as they made their way slowly through the slushy, melting ice and in that direction.

Just before they arrived, Cameron held everyone back as he peeked around the corner and recognized what looked like Brian's body hanging. He immediately backed away from the corner of the ice wall street and took a deep breath as he whispered, "Man, that is just sick. I can't believe what they've done to him. The people we were fighting in Afghanistan never did anything as bad as that to any of our soldiers."

When Cameron saw Brian, he was hanging upside down from one of the old, non-working traffic lights in what used to be the town's main street. Two soldiers were laughing and gloating over their captives. One of their soldiers lay dead, not too far away, and he had two arrows in him from Brian's bow. Cameron choked out the whispers, "Looks like Brian may have followed one of the soldiers in here and decided to kill him, and that's how he got so deep into enemy territory. He wasn't counting on being ambushed by the other two soldiers."

Rachel had to look for herself as she moved forward and peeked around the corner. Seeing Brian, she said, "Those fucking bastards have skinned him alive." Brian's feet were tied, and he was hanging upside down by a rope with his hands dangling toward the ground. His blood was spattered all over the white ice beneath his body. The soldiers had cut him at the ankles. They peeled his skin down and away from his body, and all while he was still alive. His limp body was now jerking as he was taking his last breath.

It was such a gruesome sight that Rachel let out a gasp and said in a low, angry whisper, "Those scumbags, how could anyone do that to another human being. That's just so damn inhumane." Right after she said that, she instantly bent over and threw up; Rachel had to cup her hands over her mouth to keep from giving away their position. Cameron tried to comfort her as he moved up close to her and put his arm around her shoulders.

Cameron then quickly looked around to ensure the soldiers hadn't heard her or seen them hiding in the dark street shadows. They were waiting a few minutes, seeing that the soldiers occupied themselves in the glory of their kill. The soldiers didn't hear or spot the group.

Cameron whispered, "Ok, come on, let's circle and get up close so we can kill those soldiers. Let's use our bows and arrows to bring the entire enemy soldiers down on us. He directed Rachel, Aron, and Thomas to move in a direction like he would have done one of his squads in Afghanistan under his command. "The three of you will take the next street to the north while Staci and I will take the one to the south. Let's try getting as close to them as possible, but give us about ten minutes to get into position. I'll signal you by having Staci raise her left arm. Once she drops her arm, then take your shots." Everyone shook their heads in agreement as they understood their orders.

The two groups slowly reached where they were within thirty yards of the two soldiers.

Cameron whispered to Staci, "You take the one on the left, and I'll take the one on the right." Staci nodded her head in anger and loaded her bow. "Aim at the middle of the chest and fire after you signal." He loaded his bow, and once he saw that Thomas's group was in position, Cameron told Staci to raise her arm and give everyone the signal. Everyone's bow was ready as she dropped her arm, and the arrows flew with laser-like accuracy and met their targets. One of the soldiers let out a scream as the arrow hit him in the chest. Cameron quickly took out another arrow and reshot him while screaming and squirming on the ice. And it didn't take long, and the screaming soon ceased.

Before they made any moves, the groups waited a few long silent minutes to see if other soldiers would show up after hearing their comrade's screams. They had to ensure their enemies were out of commission and that other soldiers weren't coming to their aid before advancing toward their kill. Not seeing or getting any other enemy activity, they moved in close to the dead soldiers and Brian. One soldier was still breathing and gasping for air, so Cameron quickly walked over to him and hit him in the head a few times with the butt of his rifle. As he was hitting him, he said with clenched teeth and a low, angry voice, "This is for our buddy Brian, you peace of shit."

Before they did anything else, Cameron went over to the rope, holding Brian suspended in the air, cutting it, and slowly starting to lower his body. He told Aron and Thomas to grab and lay him between two ice mounds a few yards away. Aron took the upper body, and Thomas took his feet as they caught him before lowered into the pool of blood that lies beneath him. Cameron said, "Man, this just isn't right; those fuckers were animals." "As he moved up closer to the two dead soldiers, he said, "This makes me want to go after all those low-life individuals and kill as many as we can."

He told Aron and Thomas to grab them and tie the rope around one leg of each of them, and they would string them up like they did Brian. "We should skin them as they did to Brian, but we don't have the time." After they had them tied around the ankles, the three of them slowly raised the soldiers until they could tie the rope off. Now, they were the ones that were dangling in the air for everyone to see.

Cameron said, "This will let their buddies know that we didn't let their soldiers get away with killing Brian."

They retrieved all their arrows before they left as Cameron told everyone, "Brian's dead, and there's nothing we can do for him now. We can't even give him a decent burial, so we have to leave him like that. We need to get out of here before they have more soldiers all over us. Thomas, you, and Aron will take one of the soldier's snowmobiles, and Rachel, Staci, and I will take the other one and get out of here.

Don't let the pain of losing Brian cloud your judgment. Keep your eyes and ears open for soldiers or anything that looks like an ambush. We don't want to all end up dead."

They quickly looked around to make sure no other soldiers headed in their direction and then took all the weapons from the dead men. They promptly filled their backpacks with everything they could carry. They prepared to bear back to their hideout.

The girls were softly crying as they returned to their safe place. Before arriving, they hid the snowmobiles in an ice pack and covered them with ice. Once back at their hideout, they gathered together and talked for a few hours about what had happened. With heavy hearts, they said prayers for Brian. They knew they weren't going to get much sleep that night because of the loss of Brian. It was also the first time any of the members, except Cameron, had killed another human being, and it was heavy upon their hearts. The rest of the night would be a soul-searching time for all of them. They took turns standing guard the rest of the night just in case the soldiers found their hideout and tried to sneak up on them while trying to sleep.

***

Chapter 1

In the early 1990s, the United States military started working on a secret program called "HAARP," based in Alaska. It's a high-frequency Active Auroral Research Program jointly managed by the United States Air Force and the United States Navy. Congressional records show that the United States government funds the HAARP Program. When questioned about its intended use, the United States military and federal government tried to say that the facility was once an experimental facility shut down and was no longer in operation.

It was initially designed to "understand, simulate and control ionospheric processes that might alter the performance of communication and surveillance systems. After experimenting with the program, they soon found they could change the weather over parts of the earth by utilizing the system. It didn't take long before they began experimenting with the program's use.

The HAARP system can deliver enormous amounts of electricity and energy, comparable to a nuclear bomb, anywhere on earth, using laser and particle beams. The system can beam 3.6 Gigawatts of radiated power of high-frequency radio energy into the ionosphere to create an effect in the atmosphere as dramatic as that of a thermonuclear bomb. It can knock out all radio transmission and other frequencies anywhere in the world where it gets directed. The warfare system has been better known as "eco-type terrorism" because countries now can effectively do what they call "Weather Warfare," any place on earth and especially against each other.

There are two HARP facilities in the United States, plus China and Russia each set up two replicas of the HAARP program and started experimenting with it in the 1990s. They can alter the earth's climate and set off earthquakes and volcanoes, direct a drought, hurricanes, and tornadoes, and target any place on earth they want to reach against their enemies by using the system. *

The first confirmed use of weather warfare was by the United States in South Vietnam when they seeded the clouds over the Ho Chi Minh Trail with Silver Iodide and made it rain for several weeks. The mission succeeded from 1967 to 1972.

Russia had also successfully experimented with its system several times in different parts of the world and prepared to use it. They'd been planning some invasion of the United States for many years after the Cold War ended, and this weapon seemed to be the perfect fit for their use and intent to take over complete control of the United States.

The radical President of Russia had decided he would put what he thought was his highly thought-out plan into action. He decided to utilize their "Weather Warfare System, along with a coordinated Russian ground invasion against the United States. He reasoned that the United States was justified in its military response. The American leaders were primarily unaware that the Russians could interpret their talks about democracy, human rights, personal freedom, and economic prosperity as a hybrid warfare type. The important thing was that the Russian leaders saw it as a prelude to war.

Most experts believed that Russia had no chance in a war with America and its allies. They thought the United States military and its partners would destroy the Russian army in any toe-to-toe conventional fight since the United States has many advantages over Russia. The United States has far more powerful forces, higher technology, global reach, and many more allies. Regardless, the Russian president convinced himself that America was weak, vulnerable, and unprepared for Russia's type of attack against the United States. He also believed his country's only chance of winning a war against the United States was to make the first military move.

Even though Russia decided to attack America, they believed it would not be an excellent move to use nuclear weapons. They thought that would be a losing proposition for both sides; Russia would not use the nuclear arsenal because of that. However, the Russian strategy was to try and use the threat of atomic weapons as a deterrent to convince United States NATO allies not to respond to the Russian aggression against America.

Russia's most significant military problem was that they had no severe allies to help them, except for Syria, Iran, and China. However, China had nothing to gain from a war with America, so they weren't willing to get involved with what they would soon learn was not a well-planned Russian invasion. China's interests in Russia are purely economic because they need natural resources from Russia due to its massive population and enormous demands. There is nothing military about China and Russia's relationship. Therefore, China felt it had nothing to gain by fighting a losing war against America and its allies. China knew it would prolong the war if they were to get involved, but the result would ultimately be like the United States fighting Russia alone.

Nothing could dissuade the Russian President as he pursued his secret plan. They set off a thermonuclear bomb over the United States and knocked out all communication systems. They followed-up by using the "Weather Warfare" system that unleashed a massive storm over America. They could use ocean flow snow by utilizing the ocean waters off the Pacific and Atlantic Coasts to create the snow they needed to cover America.

The massive snowstorm lasted ten days and dropped 20 to 25 feet of snow over America's surface. They immediately utilized a freezing Arctic Blast across America that lasted another eight days. It immediately froze the snow in place. Russia knew most people in America couldn't survive prolonged freezing, which was 100 degrees below zero. The cold air caused people to lose electricity and heating, weakening their survival ability. Most people on the West Coast states froze to death within the first few weeks because they weren't used to or prepared for a storm of that magnitude.

The Russian attack occurred on December 26, 2025, once the Russian troops and equipment were prepared and ready to deploy. Once they shut down the Arctic Blast over America, they used amphibious assaults on the west coast and east coast and deployed 200,000 ground troops into America.

Many older military bases in the United States have been closed and turned into detention centers over the past several years. Over 800 such camps in the United States are empty, but they are all fully operational and ready to receive prisoners, staffed, and even have full-time guards. The detention camps operate through FEMA and exist under the disguise of activation in the case of Martial Law in the United States.

There has been some reasoning that if a "mass exodus" of illegal aliens crossed the Mexican/US border, they would be quickly rounded up and detained in detention centers. However, some believe that the real reason they were set up was to hold the homeless, poor, and drug addicts scattered throughout the United States. Also, people couldn't afford to rent a home because they didn't have enough income. Instead of letting them live on the streets and alleys of the town in America like they have been doing, the government could hold them in all the empty detention camps. It would get them off the streets, and the government would also be able to control them.

The camps all have railroad facilities and roads leading to and from the detention facilities for easy access, and many have an airport nearby. Most of the centers can house a population of 20,000 detainees. Currently, the largest of these facilities is just outside of Fairbanks, Alaska. The Alaskan facility is massive and can hold approximately 2 million (2,000,000) people.

Russia believed the remaining survivors of the storm could be rounded up and put into the empty FEMA detention camps in America. They foolishly thought they would be able to control those detention camps with their already infiltrated soldiers. The Russian

President wasn't counting on it because all the detention camps would also be under ice and not fully functional as he had planned. Therefore, they had no place to hold and take care of the survivors outside of the detention centers. Once the Russian president realized his miscalculation, the only choice was to kill all the survivors they came across.

Russia had started training its KGB soldiers to infiltrate America during the cold war. The soldiers entered America, some legally and in other ways. During the "open border" policy from 2008 to 2016, many KGB personnel entered the United States on visas and never left. They all had one purpose in mind: to blend in with the general population of America. The Russian soldiers were mainly college graduates who were well-versed and trained in Western political and economic culture. They became trained at the academy known as "The Institute." Some of their training took up to a decade to complete. They become affluent in several languages, including English. They received stringent ideological secret tuition from the Russian government to cover their living expenses while in America. The Russian president planned that those soldiers were going to take over the FEMA detention camps. What he didn't realize is that most of them had become Americanized and were also killed in the massive storm because they never received an advanced warning from the Russian government that the deadly storm was heading their way.

Inside America, over 120 deep underground military bases are situated under some major cities, such as US Air Force Bases, US Navy Bases, US Army Bases, and the Department of Homeland Security control centers. Almost all these bases are over 2 miles underground and have diameters ranging from 10 to 30 miles. The inside of some of those underground bases is basically like large cities. The United States has been building these bases day and night since the 1940s.

They have connected these underground military bases using nuclear-powered subterranean machines that work by melting through rock and soil at 2000-degree temperatures and turning them into melton rock. They can drill a tunnel seven-mile-long in one day. The tunnels automatically seal and are large enough to drive military vehicles, tanks, and missiles. The bases are connected by high-speed magneto-levity trains that travel up to 1500 MPH from base to base.

Area 51 and 52 in Nevada are two bases directly connected to the Base in Denver and Washington D.C. Government. Personnel can catch one of the high-speed trains in the secret military base at Area 51 or area 52 and be in Washington, D.C., in an hour or less. Each Base has thousands of personnel and troops located inside the base.

The bases have an underground back-up system that would continue to operate even after hundreds of nuclear blasts over the United States took out all the electrical power grids above ground. The underground bases are entirely waterproof, bombproof, and, most importantly, connected to the government headquarters compound center in Washington, D.C.

Once Russia shut down the storm system, the Russian soldiers landed in America. They set up command headquarters to monitor their progress along the coastlines in the western and eastern parts of the United States. They soon started sending their soldiers out on search and destroy missions to kill all survivors they could find.

The United States still controlled its entire military and nuclear arsenal. As soon as the President of the United States found out that Russia was behind America's invasion, he tried to contact the Russian president several times. He wanted to let him know that using nuclear weapons against Russia could be available to the United States government if he didn't deactivate his troops. Unfortunately, during the first several weeks of the attack, there was no communication between the two Presidents. Realizing that conventional methods could defeat Russia, the United States President decided not to use nuclear weapons.

The United States President activated all the military missile defense systems deep within the underground bases. He ensured that all satellite shields were in place and working so an invading country couldn't destroy them. He immediately notified the United States Navy, Air Force, Army, and all the American allies in foreign countries to be on high alert for attacks from Russian missiles, planes, and possible incoming nuclear bombs.

The sea war was raging between the United States and Russia, and the United States military controlled the United States' ships, subs, and other military arsenals in the underground military bases. Russia was in an all-out war with the United States, just short of using nuclear weapons.

The United States president ordered troops from the United States bases in Alaska to move south through Canada, connect with a large portion of the underground forces, and engage Russian Soldiers. Their mission was to stop an enemy infiltrating the Western part of the United States. He also deployed amphibious ships to southern ports in the United States. Several United States ships are under the United States control for an Amphibious assault. These United States soldiers' mission was to connect with the remaining underground troops and intercept and engage Russian soldiers from the Eastern part of America.

A large portion of the American survivors of the storm were able to find places to make shelters and hide out as they continued to survive. They armed themselves with weapons and fought to protect themselves from the invading Russians that were in America. None of the survivors wanted to take up arms and fight, but It was a matter of human survival. It wasn't their intent, but by accident, so the survivors had become "Accidental Soldiers," just like Cameron and his small group. *

***

Chapter 2

After college, each of Cameron's close friends enthusiastically went their separate ways to fulfill their dreams and ambitions. The last time they were all together was just a few months earlier at their ten-year Cal Poly class reunion. It was at the reunion; they promised to meet up with each other in a few months between Christmas and New Year's and take a ski trip. They wanted to make another one of their ski trips to China Peak Ski Resort, northeast of Fresno, California, which they had done each year during college. They believed it would give them the perfect opportunity to catch up on what was going on in each other's lives and, at the same time, enjoy skiing and snowboarding together.

Cameron Journey was outgoing, popular, a good-looking guy with dark brown hair and blue eyes. He was five feet ten inches tall, had a medium build, and was a no-nonsense person who always seemed to control himself and his life. Becoming a career officer in the military appeared to be the perfect fit for him. Soon after college, he enlisted in the Army and joined the Army's Special Forces program. After several months of hard grinding training, he became an officer and graduated from officer candidate school.

Within a few years, he reached the rank of Captain and spent two tours of duty in Afghanistan. During his time in Afghanistan, he had a company of infantry soldiers under his command. When he first enlisted in the military for his initial 6-year stint, he had planned to make the Army his career. Still, after fighting the Taliban in Afghanistan and doing many soul searching, he decided the military career was not what he wanted. When it was time for him to extend his enlistment period after six years, he chose to forego the military profession.

Once, his company had several encounters in Afghanistan and killed hundreds of enemy insurgents. Several of his soldiers died, so fighting soldiers and killing people had lost its appeal to Cameron.

After his duty was over, he chose a slower pace of life and became a financial advisor in his father's firm in Fresno.

While in college, Cameron and his friends could take advantage of the generosity of a close family friend of Cameron's parents. Dr. Marvin and Janice Johnson owned a large cabin about 20 miles south of the China Peak Ski Resort in the small resort town of Shaver Lake. The Johnsons always kept it stocked with food, supplies, and wood, ready to use year-round. They let Cameron and his friends use it between Christmas and New Year's. The Johnsons trusted Cameron and his friends with the cabin and knew they would clean the place and replace the wood they used. Dr. Johnson had a deal with Cameron that he and his friends would come up during their summer break and replace the wood and gas they used during their ski trips. Cameron had plenty of friends willing to help him with that chore so he could get away for a few days and stay in the cabin. The girls joked about calling the place a cabin. At over 3,600 square feet and six bedrooms, three bathrooms were larger than most people's private homes.

Shaver Lake is in the mountains about 50 miles northeast of Fresno. At the higher elevation, it receives several feet of snow each year. Although it gets a lot of snow in the winter, it melts fast during the spring because of the warmer temperature.

The cabin is in a private subdivision with many trees and a private road with several homes spread out along the street. All the lots are 2 ½ acre parcels and snow-plowed once the snow started to fall. The cabin is located at the end of the one-lane paved road and on the side of a hill. It's at the highest point in the subdivision and has excellent views down toward the Central Valley. The back of the house faces west, so you can see miles down the canyons and enjoy picturesque views. Most nights, when it's clear, you can look down at the valley towns where the lights shine like millions of sparkling stars in the night skies.

The cabin stands off the ground, and the first floor is about 10 feet from the ground. When you turn into the driveway, you go up and around in a half-circle about 100 feet and turn left into a three-car garage on the same first-floor level as the house. It has an A-frame roof, and at the peak, it is approximately 50 feet from the ground floor. The A-frame top helps keep the snow off the cabin's roof during winter. The living room has high windows looking at a fully covered wooden deck. There is also a massive rock fireplace in the big open living room where you can sit on a rock seat by the fire.

Underneath the garage, a door opens to the outside of the cabin, making it easy to store the wood and snow equipment. It has a lift door in the garage with stairs leading down to the lower level. It was easy to get the wood when it was snowing or raining outside without getting wet. The Johnson's kept it stocked with at least five cords of wood. Two sets of snowshoes and cross-country skis are hanging on the wall in the garage just in case someone decides to hike in the snow. It contains two generators and a whole five-gallon gas can if an emergency occurs.

During this ski trip, Cameron secured the cabin with the Johnsons for the day after Christmas. Once he knew they had the place, he coordinated the ski trip with his friends. They planned to meet at Cameron's parents' house in Fresno, drop off their vehicles, and then take only two to the cabin.

One of the guys with Cameron was Thomas Martin, who had become Cameron's best friend in college. They kept in touch with each other and talked as often as they could after college. He graduated with a degree in Agriculture and worked on his family's orange orchards in Ivanhoe, California. His family owned approximately a thousand acres of citrus, and his father always wanted Thomas to take over part of the family farming business someday. Once he graduated from college, he did as his father wished and became a more significant part of the day-to-day farming operations.

He had wavy light brown hair, stood five feet eleven inches tall, and weighed 175 pounds, thin but strong. He was always laughing and joking with his friends.

Once established on the farms, he married a girl he'd attended high school with and dated during college. They had two young boys, ages 2 and 4, so his wife decided to stay home on this trip but told him to have fun on the ski slopes with his friends.

He asked his mom and dad to keep an eye on his wife and kids while he was gone and had his dad watch the ranches to make sure the oranges didn't freeze while he was gone. It sometimes got down to below 32 degrees freezing temperatures in the valley during that time of the year, and even though they had wind machines on the property, he didn't want to lose the entire orange crop from a long, hard freeze just because he was having fun on the slopes with his friends.

Once everyone was at Cameron's place, they shook hands, hugged, and loaded up their things in Cameron's SUV and Thomas's Range Rover. As they headed up to the cabin, they were excited. They joked and laughed during the entire two-hour ride up into the mountains.

When they got to the cabin, they parked in the driveway and jumped out of the vehicles, and Cameron stretched out his arms in the air toward the sky and spread his feet apart as he breathed in the cold fresh air. "Mab, I love the smell of those pine trees. I'd forgotten how good and fresh everything smells up here. I don't think I'll ever get tired of this place. I can't believe how much I've missed being here."

Thomas chuckled and said, "Yeah, me too. Being up here brings back a lot of good memories for all of us." After a few minutes, they opened the garage doors and parked the two vehicles inside.

They took time to unpack the cars and bring in their items, and once everyone was comfortable, they settled in by the fireplace. They lit the wood in the fireplace and built a fire. They were starting to relax as they cozied around the warm fire. The guys had their beers, and the girls had their glasses of wine. They continued to laugh and joke for a few hours and catch up on what each other had been doing since they had graduated from school. It was like old times, and they felt comfortable with each other's company again.

One of the two girls in the group was Staci Corcoran, a cheerleader at Cal Polly for four years. She was blond and five feet five inches tall with a slender build. She had a bubbly personality and was easy to talk to and to like. She landed a great job as a pharmaceutical sales representative in Los Angeles a few years after college. She had been married for a few years but had recently gone through a nasty divorce. Being single again, she welcomed the opportunity to try and get away from her hectic life and clear the cobwebs in her head. She also knew it would be an excellent time to enjoy the company with her old friends. She hadn't seen Cameron for several years before the class reunion, and deep inside, she was secretly looking forward to seeing him. She hoped they could have time to talk, be alone, and maybe reconnect. She and Cameron dated each other for their last two years in college but never had real closure with each other. The deal-breaker in their relationship was that she didn't like him becoming a career soldier and a career soldier's wife. Staci didn't want to be left alone for months in a foreign country. She had never gotten over him and still had a lot of strong feelings for him. She wanted to see if there was still something between the two of them.

Later in the evening, they noticed it had started to snow and was heavy. The guys laughed about it at first, as Thomas half-jokingly said, "I don't think we'll be able to go snowboarding or skiing tomorrow with the way that stuff is coming down. Unless it eases up at night, we better get our playing cards out for the next few days." None of them realized what was in store for them. They continued to have a little more beer and wine, enjoying their time together and away from home. They were enjoying talking about old times.

It was around midnight before they finally decided to call it a night. Cameron went outside to check the snow before bed, but the massive storm wasn't letting up. There were high winds, and you could hear it howling through the trees like a freight train as the snow came down about two inches per hour.

Staci felt uneasy because of the noise and the high winds whooshed through the giant pine trees. She was afraid it might blow one of them down on the cabin, so she was sitting up in bed with her legs pulled up toward her chest and her arms wrapped around her legs. Staci couldn't sleep and nervously bit her fingernails. Cameron checked on her before he went to bed and saw that she was freaking out, so he went and sat down next to her on the bed. He put his arm around her to try to reassure and comfort her.

They talked for about an hour, and he told her he was deeply hurt when they broke up. He said he loved her very much and still had deep feelings for her. She was happy to hear that and told him she felt the same way. He told her he didn't understand at the time why she didn't want to be part of the military life. He said he finally understood after being in the service for a while. Cameron told her that after he had been in the military for a few years, he realized he didn't want to make it his career either. However, he told her that one of his biggest concerns was feeling apprehensive about starting a relationship with her again. He didn't want to get hurt by her again. She told him she understood how he felt and hoped it wasn't too late for them to try again. She said she'd never leave him again if he gave her another chance. He told her he would think about that over the next few days and see how things go. They hugged and kissed before he went to his room.

Cameron stayed awake and thought about some of Staci's words. Seeing and being with her brought back some of his old feelings for her, making him realize he still loved her. Cameron wasn't sure if he could trust her to not do that again to him if things didn't go the way she wanted. After all, she had left him once before because she disagreed with his career choice. Cameron felt at the time that if Staci loved him, she would've stayed with him regardless of what he chose to do. Although he now understood some of her reasoning, he still wasn't sure he could trust her, saying she would be willing to commit to him again. After giving it a great deal of thought, he decided to sleep on it and see if he could find out if her feelings toward him were sincere and honest over the next few days.

It wasn't long before the group lost all their cell phones and other electronic power connections. At that same time, they also lost all the electricity in the cabin, which would have left them without running water if it hadn't been for the two backup generators below the garage. Cameron and Thomas started hunting around for flashlights and candles. Once they found them, they were able to get one of the generators running. Now they had electricity and especially heat for the night once again. They watched it and ensured it worked before returning to bed to catch some much-needed sleep.

Cameron was used to getting up early in the Army because he would get up at five in the morning and be ready to meet up with his soldiers. He was the first one up in the early morning hours. Brian got up early at the dairy and milked the cows, so he was behind Cameron. They'd gone outside several times to check the snow conditions and found the snow hadn't eased up. Cameron made a large pot of coffee for everyone as he and Brian sat at the kitchen table and talked for a while before everyone else finally started crawling out of bed. As the rest of the group made it to the kitchen area, Brian said, "I don't think any of us are leaving the house today. We got about two feet of snow during the night, and it's still snowing hard and heavy. If we could get to the slopes, we couldn't ski or snowboard in this stuff. You can only see a few feet in front of your nose."

Brian Parker was Cameron and Thomas's good friend, and they had been roommates during their last two years in college. He also graduated with a degree in Agriculture and worked on the family dairy farm near Sacramento once he graduated. He had worked on the dairy since he was a young boy, so returning to it after college was natural. He was now a big guy, about six feet, two inches tall, and two hundred pounds. Thomas teased him that he could lift a hundred-pound hay bale over his head with one arm and then toss it 20 feet. He had a few girlfriends in college but never settled down to just one girl. Maybe it was because girls thought he was shy and didn't talk much unless someone asked him a question or felt he had something important to say. He always seemed as though he was deep in thought when he was around people, especially girls. He appeared to be a loner, but Cameron and Thomas knew he really wasn't and would always tease him about being so severe all the time. Thomas always called him Mr. Serious.

Thomas wore sweatpants and a sweatshirt as he opened the back door and walked out onto the covered deck. The visibility past the overhang of the patio roof was almost zero. As he squinted his eyes, he was still unable to see past the. As he hurried back inside, he closed the door behind him and shivered.

He had a little fear in his voice as he said, "Crazy, I've never seen it drop that much snow in one night; that's just unbelievable.

You're right, Brian. We can't go anywhere in that stuff." Little did they know then, but the Russian Weather Warfare Storm had begun, and conditions would worsen for all of them.

As they had their coffee, they talked about what they would do if it kept snowing like it was for the next few days. Cameron told everyone that he felt they were stuck there, and maybe for a lot longer than just the weekend trip they had planned. He said, "If the generators fail, we'll have to start boiling snow to have water to drink and keep a bucket of water to pour into the toilets after we use them. If the generators fail, the toilets and pipes will freeze and burst. We could be in a real predicament, so we must keep the generators going. If one fails, then we'll start up the other one.

I don't think we've ever seen anything like this in all the years we've been coming up here."

Staci looked a little wide-eyed and frightened as she said, "Hey Cameron, that stupid wind is still blowing hard, and it's scary. What do we do if it blows one of the large pine trees down on us?

Cameron replied, "We better pray that won't happen."

Thomas said, "Yeah, we must also pray this stuff stops soon to get home. I don't want to be stuck up here very long." Rachel shrugged her shoulders and raised her eyebrows as if in doubt. The snow was going to slow down any time soon. It was almost like she knew something the rest of them didn't, but she didn't.

While sitting together, they had an uneasy feeling that there was something much different about this storm. Everyone looked at each other with puzzled looks on their faces. This storm wasn't expected because they had checked the weather reports several days before they planned the ski trip, and it was nowhere on the radar. There wasn't even a hint of anything that resembled a storm of this magnitude.

Thomas typically made jokes and had fun with everyone, but he was now serious and having difficulty sitting still because he knew his wife would be worried about him. He nervously got up and went outside to check out the snow and see if there was any possibility the storm might be letting up soon. While outside, Thomas checked his phone once again to see if he could get any reception, but not getting anything, he started thinking about finding a way to get home to be with his wife and kids. He believed the vast storm must've knocked out a satellite, so they weren't getting any reception.

Once back inside, Thomas said, "Hey guys, I feel bad about this storm. I don't think this stuff will let up for a while; it's coming down in buckets. I will go down the road and see if anyone uses snowplow equipment. I want to see if anyone can help us get out of here. See if we can make it to the main road." Cameron told him he would go with him as they went to the garage, got the snow shovels, opened the garage door, and dug a pathway to the top of the snow.

Everyone was standing in the garage when Cameron told the rest of the group they would check things out. Thomas and Cameron put on the snowshoes and made their way out onto what once was the one-lane road. Everything was covered in fresh, deep snow. They went about a hundred yards down the hill before they started getting a little disoriented and had to stop. Their visibility was only a few feet because of the strong winds and the heavy snow falling. Fearing they might get lost if they went further down the road, they returned to the cabin before they couldn't find their way back. Thomas yelled out, "This is ridiculous!"

There was no way they could drive a car through that much snow and under those conditions. The snow was too deep and soft to get one out of the garage. You also couldn't see where you were going, even if you could drive a car in the falling heavy snow. When they returned, they told the rest of the group that they could not get down the main road and out of the mountains. They informed everyone they were stuck in the cabin and would have to ride out the storm.

***

Chapter 3

The group continued burning wood as they huddled around the fireplace, trying to understand what was happening and what to do. Thomas was bummed he couldn't get in touch with his wife to let her know he was ok. He didn't realize that the entire valley was also getting the same amount of snow they were getting up there in the mountains. It was customary to have snow in the mountains this time of year, but it hardly ever snowed on the valley floor. The last time the central valley had snow was in 1960, and it was only a few inches, which melted within a few hours.

Rachel Duncan was also a cheerleader at Cal Polly and a good friend to everyone in the group, especially Staci. She was the one who told Staci about the ski trip and thought it would be a good time for Cameron and Staci to reconnect. Rachel was a computer whiz and extremely intelligent, fluently speaking three foreign languages: Russian, Spanish, and French. She held a high position as a computer technician for a Silicon Valley firm in San Jose, California. Five feet six inches tall with medium-length brown hair and an average-size build.

She is still single, but she had a boyfriend who was also a computer geek in the same firm where she worked. His name was Aron Freeman, and he was a few years older than her. He was about five inches taller and had a husky build. He was a little nerdy and wore thick-rimmed glasses, but he loved snowboarding and got along well with everyone in the group. He decided to take time off work and accompany Rachel on the ski trip. The two of them were almost inseparable from the first moment they met. They tried to do everything together. They had no children but planned to marry soon and start a family.

Knowing that Rachel was knowledgeable about electronics equipment, Cameron asked her what she thought about no service. Rachel said, "I don't know what is going on, but it could be a transformer that blew up, but that wouldn't knock out the power to the cell phones. It sounds like a satellite getting knocked out to me. The only other thing I can think of is that this storm is so powerful that it has interrupted the power grids that control everything in this area. I've never heard or seen of a storm that is this powerful." Even though they had electricity in the cabin because of the generator, there was no radio or television reception.

The snow continued for the next three days and wasn't letting up. They had long forgotten about skiing and snowboarding and now wondered how they would get out of this storm and back home as soon as they could to their jobs and family. Cameron said, "We don't know how long this storm will last, so we need to prepare ourselves in case it continues for a while. We need to bring in as much wood from under the garage as possible and pile it in the corner of the living room because we need to keep a fire going all the time. It's getting colder outside, and if the generators stop working, the fireplace will be the only way for us to stay warm.

It's been snowing so hard and long; there are already about four feet of snow piled up out there, and it may end up covering the entire cabin if it keeps coming down like this for several more days. We need to use the generator sparingly to avoid running out of fuel. We only have about 4 gallons left. Keeping a little heat in the house will keep the pipes and toilets from freezing and allow them to continue working. Let's keep digging a path out the back of the garage to the top of the snow every morning. That way, we can ensure we can get in and out of this stuff once it lets up." Everyone agreed, giving them something to do instead of just sitting around and wondering what was happening with their loved ones. They put several sheets down in the corner of the living room and piled half the wood on them.

It continued to snow for the next ten days, not letting up until it suddenly stopped. By then, the snow was approximately 25 feet deep outside the cabin and covered it halfway up. They could no longer look down the canyon toward the valley floor because too much snow was on the deck. Little did they know, but the snow was also 20 to 25 feet deep all over America.

It was the middle of the day when it finally stopped snowing, and everyone got together and waited with hopeful anticipation that it wouldn't start up again. After a few hours of no more snow showers, they began to feel like the storm may be over. They were moving about the cabin, hoping and praying it had passed.

Everyone had already started to get cabin fever. The group played poker, solitaire, and other games to try and occupy their time until they got burned out on all the games. They told every scary story they could remember and even sang 99 bottles of beer on the wall.

Just as suddenly as the snow stopped, the outside temperature instantly plummeted. Within several hours, the snow had frozen in place, and the outside temperature had dropped to over a hundred degrees below zero. The Cabin started cooling to freezing, even with the fireplace's heat and wood burning. The only warm place in the cabin was in front of the fireplace.

Not knowing how cold it would get inside the cabin, Cameron said, "Come on guys, let's make a fort-like the ones we used to make at home when we were kids right in front of the fireplace." Everyone pitched in as they used the couches and mattresses from the beds and made a cave-like fort before the fireplace. The girls gathered all the blankets and sleeping bags and threw them in and on top of the fort. Once they finished, Cameron figured they could spend their time in the fort and under the covers if it continued to get colder. He also believed it would help them use each other's body heat to stay warm once they snuggled next.

The gasoline was getting low in the generator, so Cameron said, "We can knock a small hole in my car's gas tank and let the gas drain into the gas can. We can plug the hole until we need more. If we do that, we won't have to worry about running out of gas for the generators. I also have an extra quart of oil in my trunk if we need it for the generators. I don't know what's happening, but we've got to do whatever we can to keep the generators running, and we have no choice but to keep the fire in the fireplace. No matter what happens, we can't let the fire burn out. It appears to keep getting colder here and must be below zero, even with the fire burning and the generator going.

Thomas said, "I've never felt this cold before, not even on the coldest nights in the orange groves. It reached 17 degrees one night, much colder than that night."

Cameron told everyone they needed to keep the fireplace heat in the living room and only one bathroom in the central part of the house and not let it escape to the other rooms. Cameron went over and closed all the doors to the other rooms. He also closed off all the vents to the other rooms. "Let's go downstairs, bring up the rest of the wood, and pile it in the corner. That should hold us for several days in case we need it."

Everyone entered the garage, reusing the wood and putting it in the room's corner. Every time they had to open the trap door to get wood, they felt the deep freeze of the air outside.

Rachel had an armful of wood as she said, "I can't believe how cold it is out there. It goes right to your bones." She stopped for a minute and continued, "Look at my breath." She blew out her breath, and it was like a fog mist.

Aron replied, "You're right; it's cold as hell. I feel stuck in a storm in Alaska or Siberia somewhere."

Over the next few days, the guys checked the outside weather to see if anything had changed. It was almost unbearable each time they went outside the protection of their homemade fort. Their nose and ears would freeze and fall off whenever they went outside. It felt like daggers going down their throat when they breathed in the air. They couldn't stay outside for more than a few seconds at a time before having to rush back in. As cold as it was in the cabin, it seemed three times that cold outside. There was no way they could tackle the Arctic blast that had paralyzed America outside the safety of the cabin.

They talked about it and knew they had no choice but to ride out the crazy storm. Even with the generator going and the fireplace putting out heat, it was still freezing inside the cabin.

At one-point, Staci screamed in frustration, "What the hell is going on with this stupid cold? This stuff is crazy. I'm so cold I don't want to get up to go to the bathroom anymore."

Cameron said, "Come over closer to me, and I'll try and keep you warm." Everyone else was feeling the same way.

Rachel said, "If this keeps up like this for several more days, then we're all screwed. It will kill us all."

Cameron said, "Come on, guys, we can't give up. We have to hang in there. Hopefully, it won't be much longer."

During the 8th day of the deep freeze, both the generators froze up and would no longer work. The guys tried to get them started again but couldn't. The only heat they had in the cabin was from the wood they had stored in the corner. They had already gone through half of what was left and hoped they had enough to last until this storm ended. Fearing the worst, Cameron said, "If we run out of wood, we'll break up everything in the house made out of wood and burn it if we have to."

Once the generators were down, they all stayed bundled up and wrapped around each other inside the fort to keep from freezing to death. They were staying covered and nuzzled up close to each other.

At one point, Rachel said, "Aron, I hope that's your foot in my crouch and not someone else's."

Thomas couldn't help himself as he jokingly said, "No, Rachel, that's mine, not Aron's."

Aron said, "Yes, it's my foot, Rachel, sorry." Everyone laughed. Maybe even a little louder and longer than they usually would, but this was one of the first times they had laughed aloud since the storm had become so severe. They were all scared and afraid they wouldn't survive the storm.

They only left the warmth of each other's warm bodies to grab something to drink, eat, or go to the bathroom. It was just pure hell and misery crawling out of their comfort area.

After several more days of trying to stay warm, Staci said, "I don't think I want to live much longer under these conditions. If this freezing temperature keeps up, I'm dead."

Cameron replied, "Come on, Staci, we all need to stay alive for each other; don't give up on me."

Staci said, "I won't give up as long as you're next to me, but I'm just sick of this stuff. There doesn't seem to be any end in sight."

Everyone started talking about what to say to loved ones if they didn't make it, and one of the group members was a lone survivor.

Finally, on the ninth day of the arctic blast, it abruptly ended. After a few hours, it slowly warmed up in the Cabin. It was none too soon for all of them. At first, everyone was a little skeptical. As the Cabin continued to warm up, there were whoops and hollers of joy from the group. They were happy that they had all made it through the storm alive. The air outside the Cabin had also returned to normal, and the ice immediately began to melt.

After spending a halfway comfortable night for the first time in almost three weeks, the guys decided to explore outside and see how things looked. They also decided to go to several neighboring cabins down the hill and see if they could talk to other survivors. Anxious to get out of there, they thought maybe they could figure a way out of the mountains.

Once outside the cabin, they finally saw the devastation the massive storm had caused. There were fallen trees everywhere that had collapsed under the weight of the ice clinging to them. As they looked further down what used to be the narrow road, they saw several collapsed roofs of the neighboring cabins. The only ones that hadn't collapsed were the ones that had an A-frame roof.

Dressed in their snow-boarding clothing and long-johns, they took shovels and snow removal equipment and headed toward the collapsed homes. They were optimistic as they hunted for survivors of the storm.

Just as they got ready to check it out, they were excited to see too little Chipmunks scurrying around and searching for food. Cameron yelled for the rest of the group to come and look. The group was elated that some animals had somehow miraculously survived the storm. Thomas said, "Can you believe those little guys survived that storm? That's unbelievable; I wonder where they could hide and stay warm enough to live through it all." Everyone was excited to see some signs of life.

The top layer of the ice was already starting to get wet, slippery, and dangerous. The guys slowly made their way down to the first cabin. It belonged to Mark and Sally Baker, who were also from Fresno. They were in their mid-sixties, and their cabin used to be their second home. They had been spending increasingly more time at their cabin than at their Fresno home. Cameron had met them several years earlier during one of the group's ski trips. He thought they were a lovely couple, and they even had him and a few guys over for dinner one night when they were replacing the wood they had used in the cabin over the winter.

It was completely frozen when they got to the house, and part of the roof collapsed from the ice's weight. The guys found the front door and started digging toward it. Even though the snow had turned to ice, it wasn't hard-packed ice like the glacier ice, and it was easier to dig through it. After searching for about ten minutes, they finally reached the front door. They tried to open the door, but it was frozen to the rest of the house and wouldn't budge. They dug through the ice to one of the windows leading to the living room. They busted it open with their shovels and entered the house.

Cameron was calling out to the Bakers as they made their way inside. It was completely dark inside, and they had to use their flashlights to see where they were going. Everything in the house was frozen, and it was still cold inside. Not getting a response from the Bakers, they slowly went through the house, searching every room until they came to the main bedroom. A couple of sleeping bags and several blankets were lying on the bed. Cameron went over and slowly pulled the frozen covers back. Mark and Sally were lying in bed, wrapped in each other's arms and completely frozen.

Cameron quickly dropped the blankets, jumped back, and said, "Holy crap. They froze to death." As Cameron backed away, Brian and Thomas each pulled down the cover to look.

Thomas said, "Hey Cameron, do you think this is what we'll find with all the cabin owners we come to?"

Cameron replied, "I sure hope not, but I think we should check out a few more cabins down the hill before we head back and talk to the girls."

They went further down the hill and dug into three more cabins. It was dark in each cabin they entered because the house was covered in ice outside, except for the chimney sticking out above the partially flattened houses. They found the same thing with two more owners, Mark and Sally Baker. Everyone was dead and frozen, and they laid down one last time. After the last discovery, Cameron said, "We need to get back to the cabin and let the girls know what we've found because this is just crazy."

On the way back, Cameron had a mind-blowing reality that struck him, thinking maybe this could be the same in the valley. When he looked down toward the valley floor, everything was white, but he wasn't sure if it was clouds or ice. He knew that traditionally, it got much colder in the mountains than in the valley, but this was no ordinary storm.

He whispered, but not where Thomas and Brian could hear him, "I wonder if my mom and dad are still alive." Thomas and Brian weren't saying much, so Cameron figured they probably thought the same about their families.

When they returned to the cabin, the girls were anxious to hear what the guys had found. Once inside, Cameron spoke up and told them that everyone they found in their cabins was frozen to death. The girls stood there for a minute, mouths open and stunned by what he said. They couldn't believe what they were hearing. They knew they had been through hell and back, trying their best to survive, and everyone was feeling lucky and thankful to God that they had made it through the storm alive, but this news was devastating.

Rachel said, "Are you kidding me? How in the hell did we get so lucky?"

Cameron said, "If we hadn't been in this cabin with the generators and all the wood, we would've all died too. We helped each other stay alive."

Everyone was standing around, stunned and shaken, when Cameron said, "I think we should go to the houses we went to today and try and retrieve as much food as we can and get a few guns, ammo, and anything else we think we might need for survival. There are survivors out there. We don't know what we may have to deal with here. We also don't know how long we will be here; I would like to see if we can find a few houses around here with a couple of snowmobiles. Maybe we can use them and start going down the valley to check on family members. I want to check on my family, and I know Thomas is worried about his family, too. We'll get some sleep tonight, and then we'll go on our hunt tomorrow."

They were quiet that night as they reflected on what had happened and what may be in store for them. They all had thoughts of whether their loved ones were still alive. Later that night, after everyone went to bed, soft sobs were coming from the girls as they feared their families and their own lives. Cameron heard them crying, so he quietly said, "Hey girls, we've made it through the worst part of the storm, so we'll be okay. Let's all say a prayer for our loved ones and hope they also survived. We don't know anything yet, so let's not invite heartache until we know." He wasn't sure what lay ahead, but he was trying to comfort the girls and maybe himself.

The following day, they were up early, wearing empty backpacks and ready to search for the things they felt they could use on their journey to the valley floor. The guys brought everything out of the houses as the girls waited at the top of the ice. The girls didn't want to see the frozen bodies, so they wouldn't go inside. They picked up canned foods and other items as they filled the backpacks.

They were also searching for some snowmobiles as they went from house to house. They knew they couldn't just walk out of the mountains because they would never make it. Even though it was only about 60 miles, walking in the heavy ice and dangerous icy conditions would be impossible.

After searching for a few days, they finally found three snowmobiles in garages in what they were now calling "Coffin Houses." They spent almost all day digging them out and putting them on the top of the ice. It took a while to get the snowmobiles working. They were still frozen from the storm. They worked on them until they were all running and in good condition. They were like new because none of them had a lot of hours on them. They were very proud of themselves as they pulled them up to the cabin and showed them to the girls.

The night before leaving the cabin, Cameron had the group make careful plans as they took an inventory of what they were taking with them. They ensured they had plenty of matches, food, shovels, rope, and other supplies as they loaded the snowmobiles.

It was early in the morning, and before they left, they stopped momentarily and said a prayer. At the end of the prayer, Cameron said,

"Thank you, Doctor and Mrs. Johnson, for saving our lives by letting us use your cabin."

They headed down the narrow-frozen road and had to go around several fallen trees as they slowly walked out of the mountains.

Staci couldn't help herself and had to say something to Cameron as she said, "See all those fallen trees? That was what I feared would happen to our cabin that first night when the wind blew so hard."

Cameron said, "I know. I wasn't sure about it either, but I didn't want to scare you any more than you were already."

She sarcastically replied, "Thanks a lot. That makes me feel a lot better."

Cameron and Staci were on one snowmobile, Aron and Rachel on another, and Thomas and Brian on the one bringing up the rear. They had filled the 5-gallon gas tank and strapped it to one of the snowmobiles as they left the security of the cabin. They knew it would be a slow trek to the valley floor because of the icy conditions of the top couple of layers of ice getting a little slippery as it melted from the sun's heat. Once they left the subdivision, they made it onto the main road pathway of highway 168, heading west toward Fresno.

***

Chapter 4

They had been in the cabin for almost three weeks and were anxious to get out of there and see their family members. Cameron suggested they go to his mom and dad's home first. They were the closest location to all the family members. He told the group they could stay with his mom and dad until they figured out what was happening.

During their trek down from the mountains, they were apprehensive and careful as they managed to make it about 20 miles when they spotted smoke coming from a lone cabin about a mile off the main road. They pulled over and talked about the smoke and now believed there must be other survivors who made it through the storm. It was the first sign of human life since the storm's end, and they were excited to talk to whoever was inside. They agreed to go in the direction of the smoke. They wanted to talk to the people about how they had survived.

When they got close to the cabin, they could tell the entire house was covered in ice except for the A-frame roof that stuck up like an Indian TP above the ice. It had a chimney that had white smoke slowly drifting up into the blue sky coming out of it. As they approached the entrance, they saw the survivors dug a path from the cabin's front door to the top of the ice. Without regard for their safety, the group pulled the snowmobiles close to the opening, shut them off, and quickly jumped off. They were excited to talk to the people inside.

Cameron started yelling below to see if anyone heard them drive up and would answer his calls. After a few minutes, a very cautious middle-aged man came out of the door below, holding a rifle firmly in his hands. The guy wasn't friendly at first, which surprised Cameron and Thomas. They thought he would be happy to see someone else who survived the storm beside themselves. It appeared he was a little angry that they had intruded into his privacy. It didn't even occur to them that maybe he was a little afraid of them and what they might do to him and his family. Cameron and Thomas didn't realize the guy was worried they were there to rob him or kill him and his family.

Cameron and Thomas immediately put their hands in the air, and Cameron said, "Hey, mister, we saw your smoke and realized someone besides the six of us had survived the storm, and we just wanted to talk to you and find out how you survived. A group of us was on a ski trip and staying in a cabin at Shaver Lake when the storm hit. Somehow, we all made it through that entire screwed-up storm."

The guy looked as though he was bewildered as he slowly said, "So, how did you make it through those freezing temperatures?"

Cameron replied, "It wasn't easy. We burned almost five cords of wood and alternated the two generators until they finally froze up on us after the 8th of below-freezing temperatures. We kept the firewood burning twenty-four hours a day, and we made a cave out of the couches and beds and kept bundled up close to each other right in front of the fireplace the entire time. How about you? How did you make it?"

The guy quickly shrugged off what Cameron had just said as he said in a slow, gruff voice, "So you're not here to try and steal our food or kill us?"

Cameron was a little taken aback by him saying that and replied, "Hell no, we have our food, and we don't want to hurt anyone. We're just a group of old college friends on a ski trip, and we got trapped in a cabin at Shaver Lake. We just wanted to find out about how you survived the storm, that's all. We don't want to hurt anyone."

The guy slowly lowered his rifle and said, "If you would like to, you could have your group come on down, and I'll have my wife make us a pot of coffee so we can talk about everything."

Once inside, a shy, middle-aged, thin, and fragile-looking woman slowly emerged from one room. She seemed a little scared, or maybe she was a little embarrassed to have guests, but the group couldn't tell which.

She had a slight smile on her face as she quietly said, "I can't believe you kids survived that storm. It was horrible. We've been looking around at our neighbors' homes the past few days for survivors and haven't found anyone else alive. You're the first people alive we've seen."

Cameron replied, "We were lucky we were at a large cabin that had two generators we used and a lot of wood we could burn. That, plus relying on each other, kept us alive."

Staci spoke up and asked, "So, how did the two of you survive?"

The guy's voice now had changed, and he wasn't the gruff, angry guy he'd been outside as he said, "My name is Jerry, and this is my wife, Ann. We just got lucky, but we live here full time and did the same thing as you kids. We had several cords of wood for the winter, so we had plenty to burn. We burn it almost daily in these mountains, keeping us alive. We also had a generator that helped us for a while, but I think if that severe cold would've lasted a few more days, I don't think we'd made it much longer."

When he said that, Staci replied, "I said the same thing about three days ago. I was starting to worry that it would never get warm again."

Cameron told them his family was from Fresno, and Thomas's family was from Ivanhoe, and they wanted to get down to the valley floor and see if they could find their families and let them know what had happened to them.

Jerry replied, "If the rest of California and the valley has this much snow and it got that damn cold, I doubt very seriously if many of the people in the valley survived that storm. Especially since California won't let people use their fireplaces down on the valley floor, and they don't have wood stored up to burn as we did. When this much ice starts to melt, it will break every dam in California, and the entire valley will flood, and it will be like a huge fishbowl. You better get down to check on your family, then get out of there. I hate to tell you this, but I think the entire valley floor has ice, just like this area up here. You must prepare yourselves that not very many people were able to survive that storm, and maybe not even your family members."

That was a little hard for them to hear as they looked at each other with a startled look. They hadn't wanted to face the possibility their loved ones may all be dead. "You also need to be careful along the way because there may be survivors out there who want to rob you of everything you have and are willing to kill you for it."

Staci was shocked to hear him say that as she said, "Do you think the entire valley is covered in ice like it is here?"

Jerry replied sternly again, "Yes, I do, and I think the entire state is covered in the stuff. I wouldn't get your hopes up too high about finding surviving family members."

Staci had tears in her eyes as she said, "That's just a sad thought and too hard to try and believe or comprehend right now. It's also hard to believe people would kill us for the few things we have. I suppose we do have some things we don't want to give up, especially snowmobiles. Other survivors would probably love to get their hands on them."

Jerry said, "That's right; if they want them, they'll kill you for them for sure."

Everyone seemed in a state of shock as Rachel said, "That's an unbelievable thought." Cameron just shook his head with disgust.

They stayed for a while just talking to Jerry and Ann before Cameron said, "Thank you for your hospitality, but we have to get on down out of these mountains and see what we can find out about our family members while we still daylight so we can find my mom and dad's home." They shook hands, hugged each other, and said their good buys as they wished each other luck.

They regrouped at the top of the ice and talked about some of the scary things Jerry had said. They decided they would be a little more careful the next time they ran into some of the survivors.

Cameron said, "I never imagined some of the things Jerry was saying could happen here in America. We must be a little more cautious from now on; we can't just blindly walk into a place like that again."

Thomas said, "Yeah, I don't want someone killing us for these stupid snowmobiles."

They were soon on their way down the mountain once again. When they made their way down the valley, they spotted smoke coming from a few more houses along the way, but they didn't stop to check on them. They needed to focus on their destination to get there as soon as possible. They had traveled for several hours before Cameron pulled up and said we needed to find an empty house and stay for the night. We can't reach my mom and dad's house tonight and find their home in the dark.

They spotted the rooftop of a house a little way off the main path and made their way to it. They pulled the snowmobiles close to the front and stuck the keys in their pockets. They called out for several minutes to see if anyone was home and didn't get any response. The guys took turns and dug their way down to the front door. They knocked several times, but there still was no response, so they busted the door open. They had their flashlight in hand, and Brian took the lead as they moved slowly and defensively through the house. They wanted to be careful if someone was hiding inside and thought they were intruders and opened fire on them. After going through the entire house, they found that there wasn't anyone else in the house.

They found where the firewood was kept and dug out enough to last them for the night. They rummaged through the kitchen and found canned beans and other things to make a meal. They talked about what Jerry had warned them about and were now worried about their safety when coming across survivors. They decided to take turns and ensure someone stayed awake as a guard throughout the night. Aron and Rachel volunteered to take the first 3 hours, Brian and

Thomas took the next three, and Staci and Cameron took the last three.

It was around 6:00 AM when everyone was finally up and ready to get going once again. They traveled for several hours and didn't spot other survivors for the entire day. When they arrived at the valley floor, they couldn't believe that Jerry was right, and the whole valley was covered in twenty-five to thirty feet of ice.

As they headed toward Cameron's mom and dad's house, it was almost impossible to tell one street from the other because of the deep ice. It was like being stranded in Antarctica. After searching in the area where their house was supposed to be, it took a few hours to find the home. There didn't seem to be any signs of life. There were no dugout areas in or around the front of any places. There also weren't any footprints anywhere to be seen. That's when the realization hit him, and Cameron believed it didn't look suitable for his parent's survival.

They parked the snowmobiles, and Cameron started to dig his way down to the front door. Thomas and Brian jumped in and helped him dig. By the time they got to the front door, Cameron was breathing heavily, not only from work but also from what he feared he would find inside.

They had already found several houses near the Cabin in the mountains, and everyone inside was frozen to death. He whispered to Thomas, "This doesn't look good, Thomas."

Brian said, "Step back, Cameron, and let me go first."

Once he broke open the door, he turned on his flashlight and started to stroll through the house until he came to the main bedroom. That's when he spotted a massive lump in the middle of the large king-size bed. Cameron's parents were under a mountain of still-frozen blankets and curled up in a fetal position. They had their arms wrapped around each other and were frozen to death. Cameron was right behind Brian, and when he saw his parents, he immediately fell to his knees. He started to cry for a few minutes before he regained his composure.

He tearfully told Brian and Thomas, "This is just sick man. How could something like this happen to my family? It sucks; we can't even give them a decent burial. Everything is too frozen even to dig a grave."

He talked to Thomas and decided they would wrap the bodies up in the blankets and put them in the trunk of his dad's car. He wasn't thinking about the water that would soon be flooding the valley floor during his grief.

Rachel and Staci were softly crying as they grabbed some blankets from the linen closet and carefully helped Brian and Thomas wrap their bodies. Brian and Thomas then carried the bodies to the garage, opened the car's trunk, and carefully placed their bodies inside. It seemed to have a certain amount of privacy.

Cameron looked around and, on the nightstand next to the bed, there was a note that Cameron's dad had handwritten and left for him. It said, "Cameron if you made it through this damn storm, know that the storm was implemented by the Russians and their Weather Warfare program. Their troops will invade the United States and come in from the west and east coast with their soldiers. Be careful and look out for them because they'll try to kill you. Good luck, son. We love you with all our hearts, Mom and Dad."

After reading the letter, it suddenly made sense to the group how and why the storm lasted long and was so deadly. Everyone was perplexed about how Russia could have anything to do with the battery. They didn't know anything about the Weather Warfare program and how Russian could use it against the United States, but they had lived now through the results of them using it on America. Once the group knew what was happening with the Russians, they decided to protect themselves if they encountered the invading soldiers.

Once Cameron was in control of his emotions, he got everyone together in the living room and told them about the note she'd found and the warning his dad had left for him. Cameron said, "I don't know how Russia did it, but they did. My dad was smart when it came to stuff the government did. He once told me about this program that all the countries were working on, but I didn't believe him or pay much attention to him because it all sounded farfetched and unbelievable. I thought it was just another conspiracy theory he believed. My dad said Russia and China were working on a program like the United States had where they could direct weather in different parts of the world and any place they wanted to direct it. They could also cause earthquakes, volcanoes to erupt, hurricanes, and tornadoes. They called it the weather warfare program."

Rachel said that she had heard about the United States, China, and Russia having some warfare systems they had worked on for over 30 years.

She said, "Yes, I've heard of it. In the United States, it's called HARP, and there are two sites in Alaska. Russia could develop its version of the program and use it on us. Your dad was right, and we'll probably have Russian soldiers all over this location soon."

Staci let out a gasp, "That's just crazy stuff. I don't understand how they could make something like that happen here in America."

Aron said, "Me either, but did you ever think we'd have this much snow that quickly turned to ice here in California?"

Staci said, "So what are we going to do; there's no place to hide."

Cameron replied, "We're going to do the same thing we did in the Cabin, finding a way to survive. We'll hide out here until we get forced to move."

The house had no heat, and the group soon started breaking up all the wooden furniture and putting some of it in the fireplace to start a fire. Cameron pulled Thomas aside and talked with him.

He said, "You know you've been my best friend for most of my adult life, and I love you and your family, but we have to prepare ourselves for the fact that none of your family made it through this storm either."

Thomas didn't want to hear it but had a few tears in his eyes as he hung his head down and replied, "After what we found here with your parents, I would be surprised if any of my family survived." Thomas's younger brother was in his senior year at Cal Poly and lived with a roommate in San Luis Obispo, and Thomas wondered if he was one of the casualties of the storm as well.

They got up early the following day, and Cameron had the group head directly to the Sporting Goods store. They dug down and broke into the building, getting everything they needed to survive and protect themselves. They picked up a camping stove and propane cans to heat their food and boil water. They got battery-operated heaters, lanterns, sleeping bags, and whatever else they needed. They each got a professional bow and several arrows. They picked out a high-powered rifle and ammunition for each of them. They also tried to pick up all-white clothing they could find to wear so they would blend in with the ice.

They returned the things they needed for survival to Cameron's mom and dad's house and dropped them off before heading southeast to Ivanhoe to check on Thomas's family. It was a fifty-mile trek across the ice, but they could go straight to the property, making it a shorter distance and quicker. They could make it in a few hours.

When they got close to the ranch, Thomas could tell where the house was located because of the wind machines and tops of barns they had on the property. They were sticking up in the air and above the ice, and Thomas used them as his location points. Thomas's mom and dad's home was about a quarter-mile from his house, and the chimney was the only thing sticking out of the roof. Thomas was hoping and praying but held out little hope for the survival of his wife and kids or his mother and father.

When they arrived at Thomas's house, Cameron asked Thomas if he wanted him to go in first once they dug down through the ice to the front door. Thomas told him that he wanted to be the first one to find them if they were dead.

It wasn't long, and they had dug down to the front door, and Brian broke it open. It was like the other houses they had been in, and it was cold. Thomas's wife had also moved the mattress off the bed and put it in front of the fireplace. She had all the blankets and sleeping bags on the mattress. Thomas could tell that his wife had broken up all the wood furniture in the house and burned it in the fireplace. She also had burned all the wood he had stored outside the house, and he could tell they were alive for several days before finally losing their battle with the storm.

Thomas went over and lifted the covers from the mattress and found his wife and two children's frozen bodies. He instantly broke down and fell to his knees and leaned over and, wrapped his arms around her and the kids and screamed out "NO" in a painful, heart-wrenching scream.

Cameron also had tears when he walked over and touched Thomas's shoulder. He was very close to Thomas's wife and kids and was Thomas's best man when he and his wife married. He was also the Godfather of Thomas's son. The pain of seeing them like that cut through him like a knife. He was reliving the same pain he'd been through with his parents just the day before.

Thomas said, "We'll do the same thing with them as with your mom and dad, Cameron, but I would like to say a few prayers for them after we put them in the car's trunk."

Cameron couldn't say anything because of the massive lump in his throat, and shook his head in agreement.

The group gave him as much time as he needed to help him get through the pain until he could compose himself. After a few hours, they decided to head over to Thomas's mom and dad's house, dug down to the front door, and broke it open. Thomas found his parents wrapped around each other on a mattress before the fireplace. They were under several layers of sleeping bags and blankets. The group did the same thing with their bodies and put them in the car's trunk. They knew that would give them privacy and keep predators from getting to the bodies before the flooding water engulfed them.

They decided to spend the night at Thomas's house to have final closure with his family. The group sat down and discussed the survival of the rest of the group's families. They all believed it would be the same for their families, and they had little chance of surviving the storm. They agreed they didn't want to find their family members dead like Cameron's and Thomas's families. It was also a long distance to their family's homes, so they wouldn't travel several hundred miles to find the same result.

Cameron said, "Tomorrow morning, why don't we go back to Fresno and stay at my mom and dad's home until we can figure out what we can do to try and survive the next onslaught of the Russians? Let's all say prayers for our family members."

They were up early the following day and soon headed to Fresno. Thomas had tears in his eyes and anger in his heart as they made their way back. The group started developing a deep hatred toward the Russians for what they had done to their families. It had now become personal for them, and they had decided they were going to go on the offensive if soldiers confronted them and not just set back and let the soldiers kill them.

***

Chapter 5

It didn't take long before the Russian soldiers had infiltrated into the heart of the San Joaquin Valley of California. Getting the much-needed food for the six-member group was now getting more challenging. They were among a small number of survivalists who would soon inadvertently become accidental soldiers fighting for their mere survival against experienced Russian soldiers.

Because of his military background, the group automatically made Cameron responsible for overseeing every decision. It wasn't a job he welcomed or wanted, but he knew someone had to be in charge, and he felt his military survival training would help him keep his friends alive. He felt responsible for their wellbeing and didn't want anything happening to any of them.

After the storm ended, the group found so many dead men, women, and children inside frozen houses that the group had become calloused to all the gruesome scenes of finding people dead. Going to the Coffin Houses, they were thankful that those deceased people were helping them stay alive since most of them had stored food in their houses that the group could use for survival.

They come across the destruction and mutilation of bodies the soldiers had inflicted upon some of their captured survivors. Some survivors just gave up when they were caught by the soldiers and accepted whatever fate was in store for them. It was always a cruel and tortured death the soldiers imposed on their victims. They constantly drove their lookout snowmobiles and ATVs equipped with night vision equipment and laser beam weapons to hunt down and kill survivors who were trying their best to stay alive.

Keeping hidden without getting caught by the soldiers was becoming more challenging. Every day, it seemed like more soldiers were infiltrating into the area. For Cameron and his group, it had become like a game of cat and mouse, just trying to elude the soldiers while hunting for food. Because the ice had been melting fast, the top foot was getting slushy, and it was getting more straightforward for the enemy to track survivors, especially a group of them.

They lived in the house for about six weeks when they noticed freezing ice water that had started seeping into the bottom floor. They had a group meeting and decided to move from the house because they knew the entire valley would eventually be filled with water, which may reach several feet.

The air in the Central Valley was warming during the spring months, and it was getting up to 75 degrees during the day. It would melt much faster during the summer because the temperature sometimes would get up to 105 degrees for several days, and it even stayed hot at night. The long, hot summer lasts from June to September. The ice was melting two inches per hour on the surface. The water flowing under the ice also melts rapidly underneath the ice. At that rate, the snow may be melted entirely by the end of summer, leaving just patches of ice in different places in America. It would leave behind vast reservoirs of water, and it would take a few years for the water to dissipate.

Before the storm, the San Joaquin Valley was the world's most extensive and fertile agricultural land, producing a considerable part of the world's agriculture supply. There were three freshwater lakes in the San Joaquin Valley: Tulare Lake, Buena Vista Lake, and Kern Lake. Still, during the nineteenth century, they eventually dried up after the diversion of the Kern River. Before the storm, the San Joaquin Valley was home to approximately 4,200,000 people. The entire valley would be like a massive lake from Bakersfield to Sacramento, leaving behind millions of bodies buried under water.

The group discussed their options and thought they could move to one of the hotels in the middle of an old town, Fresno. It had several floors, and they thought it would be the perfect place for them. They believed they could stay in some higher-level rooms and be safe from the floodwaters for a few months. It was only about 6 miles away from where they had been staying, so after getting things organized, they packed everything they could carry on the snowmobiles and headed toward the hotel.

Several survivors were already hanging out there when they got to the hotel. The ice level was the same height as the top of the hotel's second floor. They parked and carefully made their way into the second-floor hallway. When they first entered the hotel, they noticed that the survivors seemed apprehensive about having anything to do with them.

Rachel stayed by the door opening and did not want a response. She told the rest of the members, "What the hell is wrong with these people? They're acting like we're their enemy?"

A young man was dressed in an American Army military uniform and standing with the survivors.

He had his rifle aimed at Cameron as he said, "Hold it right there; don't take another step, or I'll put a few holes in you. Who are you guys, and what are you doing here?"

Cameron put his hands in the air, and the rest of the group followed his response. He said, "Hey, Sargent, we're Americans, and we were up in the mountains on a ski trip when the storm hit. We've been hiding out at my parent's house here in Fresno until the water from the melting ice ran us out. We started taking on water in the house and had to move out."

After hearing their story, the soldier lowered his rifle and told them to come over to a corner of the room where they could talk privately. Cameron waived for the entire group to come on in and listen to what the Sargent had to say.

Once everyone was inside, the soldier told them what was happening. He said he was from an underground military base in area 51 located at Groom Lake in Nevada. He said he was part of a 12-man reconnaissance squad sent out from the underground base to see if there were any survivors and check and see how many Russian soldiers had infiltrated into America from the west coast. He told them the President of the United States had survived in one of the underground military facilities and controlled the United States military. He said many politicians stayed in a vast underground bunker in West Virginia. He said they were now working on defensive retaliatory efforts against Russia and directing thousands of troops who had also survived underground military bases in America. There were also American soldiers in other countries deployed back to the United States to mount an offensive against the invading Russians.

He said his squad had been ambushed in Kerman's small town, west of Fresno, by a large group of Russian soldiers, and he was the only one who survived. He said he lost all radio communication with his headquarters and was heading back to Area 51 to tell his commanding officers what had happened to his squad and about the survivors. He said he would join another American team and return after the Russians once he returned to the base.

Even though they had seen it firsthand, he told them Russian soldiers were ruthless and not interested in taking any prisoners. They're only interested in killing all survivors. He said, "You guys have been lucky so far because they've been killing people all over the west coast, including men, women, and children, and they're already here. They've set up headquarters in a different location, and they go out and search for survivors. If you stay here, they'll find you and kill you too, just like they're going to kill all of these survivors that are staying here." Cameron grimaced when he heard what the Sargent said, and now his group knew they were in big trouble. He also knew it would take time before they could get help from the American Soldiers that were going to be heading their way.

Cameron asked him, "So what does the military have planned for all of us survivors? What are they going to do to help us out?

The soldier said, "The government has plans to help everyone they can, but it is going to take time, and who knows how long it will be before the soldiers wipe out all the survivors. The government is organizing our offensive right now. I have to get back to area 51 real soon and let them know what the Russian soldiers are doing to all the survivors."

Cameron told him that he'd been a Captain in the Army Special Forces before he had recently left the service. He asked the soldier if he thought they should go with him and get back to area 51. He told Cameron he had to travel alone to return as soon as possible to let the commanders know what was happening.

Cameron asked, "Do you think we can get into the underground base at area 51 and seek protection if we go there?"

The soldier said yes if you can get there without being killed. He gave them directions on how to get there and told them, "Once you get to the base opening, you'll have to find the entrance ramp and go down to the bottom, find and push the button on the side of the external speaker and say, "Operation Turkey Neck." Once you do that, someone will let you in."

He said, "It won't be long, and we'll have American soldiers here to help protect you, but for now, you don't want to stay in this hotel because these are the types of buildings the Russians are targeting. They know this is where many survivors would like to take refuge because it's above the ice and has easier living conditions."

Cameron looked him in the eye and said, "So, what are we supposed to do? Where are we supposed to live?"

The soldier replied, "Find a place to hide or return to the cabin that saved your life. Don't just stay here like these people, or you'll end up dead. It's just a matter of time before the soldiers are here and kill everyone they find. I tried to tell them, but none of them wanted to listen. It's like they've already decided and given up."

Cameron thanked him for his information and had his group meet with him outside. They talked about what they would do for several minutes and finally agreed they didn't want to return to the cabin. Rachel suggested the group move to a spot under one of the overpasses along Highway 99. She believed they could stay there until the water under the ice got too deep. She also thought they would be safe for a while before the Russians found their hiding spot or the American Soldiers came to their rescue. That sounded like a good idea to everyone, so they left the hotel and searched along the highway until they found one of the overpass streets. They found one only a few miles from the central downtown and dug through the ice and under the overpass. Once they dug down several feet, it opened to a vast area under the overpass. They believed it was their perfect hiding place, so they set up their camp.

About a week after they settled into their hideout, they started to get low on food. It was a nice spring day, and the conditions were perfect, except for the cold emitting from the ice. They were about two miles from their hiding place in the hunt for food when a group of Russian Soldiers spotted them. Even though they were about a quarter-mile from the soldiers, one of them took a few wild shots at them. For the first time, the group experienced the aggressiveness of the Russian soldiers. The group could hear the bullets zinging through the air above their heads as they ducked for cover.

Rachel screamed out, "Those idiots are seriously trying to kill us."

Thomas yelled as he took cover, "No, kidding, they want us dead." They knew it wouldn't take long, and the soldiers would be on top of them.

The soldiers were on foot, pushing fast and hard toward their position. They watched as the soldiers headed for them. They appeared not to have any fear of Cameron's group at all. Maybe it was because Cameron's group didn't immediately return fire, and they didn't think they were armed, or perhaps they could quickly kill them like they had been doing to everyone else.

Cameron told everyone, "Ok, find a hiding place behind the ice, and let's prepare to defend ourselves. When the charging soldiers were about a hundred-and-fifty-yards away, Cameron told everyone to take careful aim at them with their automatic rifles. Several days earlier, they had talked about what they would do if they were caught out in the open by the soldiers. They quickly set up a half-circle perimeter behind a higher-layered ice shield and took cover. Everyone was about five yards apart as they loaded their weapons and readied for the Russian attack.

There were ten soldiers in the group, and they were coming at Cameron's group with the intent to kill them and not capture them. As they advanced, the group could hear them yelling in Russian. When the soldiers got within two hundred feet of their position, Cameron whistled for the group to fire. The Russian soldiers were surprised because they didn't expect much resistance from Cameron's group. The group began to pick off the soldiers, one by one, until several of them had been killed or wounded. After the initial volley, Cameron whistled for the group to cease fire and quickly retreat, not attempting to engage the soldiers further. The group gathered together and circled back to their hiding place.

When they returned, they high-fived each other and thought what a great job they had done during the fight. Everyone was whooping and hollering and proud of themselves for killing the Russians and not losing anyone in the process. It was one of the first joyous moments the group had spent with each other since they had made it out of the mountains. They had worked great as a team and deserved the joy of their efforts. It felt bizarre coming from a group of young people that, a few months earlier, would never imagine themselves in a position of killing another living being.

They had another encounter a few weeks later when they ran into a group of about fifteen soldiers heading across an open area about five hundred yards from them. They were far enough away that Cameron's group could sneak out without being detected by the soldiers. When they returned to the hideout, Cameron told the group they needed to start hunting food at night and not take any more chances during the day. He feared they would eventually get caught in an ambush during the day, and some of the group could be killed.

They began sending out a lone person to hunt for food at night. The four guys started picking straws to see whose turn it was. They had been doing it for about a month and succeeded with it before it became Brian's turn to go out alone. Cameron had already done two turns, and Thomas had one before Brian picked the unlucky short straw. Each time they went out, they were able to bring back food for the group. Although they made it back safely each time, Cameron felt that they were just lucky for not being caught or killed by the soldiers. It was during his turn to get food when the Russians killed Brian.

Brian, Cameron, and Thomas had lived together in an apartment off-campus while in school at Cal Poly and were very close friends. When Brian got killed, and, in the way, Cameron and Thomas were having a hard time accepting. It was something they couldn't wrap their heads around. They never imagined a few months earlier, while laughing and joking with each other on the first night at the cabin, that anything like that was even a remote possibility. Brian was the first one of the groups they had lost to the enemy insurgents, and they were all angry and devastated by his loss.

Killing people was something that Cameron wasn't crazy about doing when he was in the Army Special Forces, and that was the primary reason he left the military. Now, the survival instinct had kicked in and became a matter of killing or being killed for his group. The group had learned to hide during the day and savage for food and survival at night. Finding their family members dead and losing Brian had created a new mindset for everyone in the group. They now wanted to kill as many of the invading soldiers as they could. They had to be careful and pick the right time and place for a confrontation, or they would all end up dead. They agreed they would only fight the soldiers when ambushed by them, and they had no choice but to stand and fight.

***

Chapter 6

After the soldiers killed Brian and the group made it back to their hideout under the overpass, Cameron's anger was building. It had become almost overwhelming for him. The wrath boiling inside, he felt a strong desire to get even for what the Russians had done to Brian. He also couldn't get his mind off the loss of his mom and dad and Thomas's family. When he was all alone, he had tears in his eyes as he whispered, "I'm not going to let these scumbags get away with what they've done. I'm going after them as soon as it gets daylight. I will go deep into their territory and find their main camp. I'm going to kill as many of them as I can before they kill me." His anger clouded his judgment because it was the first time he wanted to get revenge against the enemy. Killing the enemy before was his military job. He also had a problem with his group's agreement, saying they would only fight when attacked.

Cameron didn't get much sleep that night because he kept replaying in his mind what he was going to do to the Russians once he caught up with them. Just as the sun started peering over the mountains from the east, he strapped his weapon over his shoulder. He was heading for his planned assault. He didn't let Thomas or anyone else know what we had planned. He knew everyone would want to come along, and he didn't want anyone feeling obligated to join him because he knew it was a dangerous suicide mission. He didn't want to lose any of his friends because of his anger and revenge.

When he got ready to leave, Staci woke up, and he told her he would be back in a couple of hours and would get the food Brian couldn't get. She sat up quickly and said, "I'm coming with you. I'll get ready in a minute and be ready to go."

Cameron kissed her and replied, "No, you stay here and get some rest. I'll be back before you know it, so get some more sleep.

"After pleading with him, she finally relented and said, "Ok, but be careful out there; I don't want anything to happen to you." Cameron thanked her and gave her another kiss before he left the safety of the hideout.

He seemed possessed as he made it to where they had stashed the two Russian Military Snowmobiles. Once he dug one of them out, he started working with the laser weapon, and it didn't take long to figure out how to use it and aim the laser at a target. He took a few practice shots at targets on the ice about fifty yards away until he felt comfortable using them. Once ready, he jumped on the snowmobile and headed toward Brian's body. As he went on his quest to hunt down the soldiers, he whispered, "Maybe the soldiers will kill me, but I'm going to get as many of them as I can before they do. I've got to do this for Brian, our families, but most of all, for my peace of mind."

As he went deeper into the old part of town, he knew he was in enemy territory because he could hear snowmobiles and ATVs buzzing in different directions. They seemed to be coming and going from a few streets over from the one he was on. Cameron figured they were sending out squads of soldiers looking for the people who killed their fellow soldiers the night before. He believed some units were returning to regroup after searching for several hours. Others were heading out on their search. He continued deeper into enemy territory until two Russian soldiers realized he wasn't wearing the standard Russian uniform. When they first saw him, they immediately began firing in his direction. Cameron instantly turned the laser weapon toward one of the guards and took him out. He quickly spun the snowmobile in a half-circle and took out the other soldier. Bullets were flying wildly all around him.

Now he realized he'd put himself in a real predicament and what he feared most. When he went around the next corner of the street, he found a large camp of soldiers that were just a few streets over from where he'd killed the two soldiers. They'd heard his skirmish with them and were preparing to go after him. When he first saw the soldiers, they looked like they were on a camping trip, with several tents and awnings in the middle of the street. They were scattered throughout the middle of the four-way intersection about four lanes over from where Brian got killed, and there were a lot more of them than he knew he could handle.

He was now so pumped from killing the soldiers that he was reacting to the moment and letting his will survive to direct him to where he was going. There was no rhyme or reason for his actions or direction.

When they first saw Cameron, they opened fire in his direction, and he quickly headed behind the corner of the nearest street. He jumped off the snowmobile but left it running. He took his automatic rifle and returned fire as he emptied two clips of 16 rounds into the soldiers before he jumped back on his snowmobile. Before leaving the area, he turned the laser gun in the soldier's direction and fired several rounds in a spray pattern into their camp. The laser beams hit several vehicles, and a few snowmobiles and ATVs burst into flames as one flew up in the air in a ball of fire.

He was trying to head out of the maze when he took one look back at the camp and knew that his initial volley from his automatic rifle and the laser gun had caused a lot of damage to the soldier's camp. He was yelling out with delight while, at the same time, he was retreating. Bullets flew in his direction as he quickly disappeared behind the street corner.

He continued to try to find his way out of the maze when he was met by a smaller squad of soldiers coming to the aid of their main camp. They were directly in Cameron's path, so as soon as he saw them, he pulled up and began firing the laser gun into the group of oncoming soldiers. Several of them went down as Cameron quickly hit the throttle, went two blocks south, and took one of the other street paths to try and get out of the maze.

He hadn't gotten far when he spotted another squad of soldiers approaching him. For a moment, he wondered if he would leave the maze alive. He thought that he might be trapped and feeling a little frantic but continued to keep his head about him and retreat and fight simultaneously. He pulled up the snowmobile again and opened a huge volley of shots from the laser gun in the middle of the charging soldiers. As the soldiers took to cover, it enabled him to disappear behind another wall of ice on one of the street paths.

Once around the corner, he again was met by a group of charging soldiers coming right at him. He made the same evasive move as the others and opened fire with his laser gun. During the brief firefight with the soldiers, his snowmobile got hit by a few incoming bullets, but it kept running. He headed down the following path south and finally found a way out of the maze. He kept looking back, but no soldiers were directly on his tail. However, he knew it wasn't going to belong. He gave the snowmobile everything it had as he continued out of the maze.

Once he felt safe, he drove the snowmobile to one of the high-rise hotel buildings and left it out front. He figured the soldiers would hunt for him at that location while he circled back on foot to the hideout. He knew the soldiers were regrouping, and it wouldn't be long before they were like a swarm of honeybees looking for him. He whispered, "It'll take them several hours to go through the buildings searching for me. By then, I'll be safe and under the overpass hideout."

Before he got back, he hid behind some ice mounds as he watched a few squads of soldiers on ATVs and snowmobiles heading in the direction of the high-rise hotel buildings. He watched them for several minutes to make sure he was out of sight of them.

On the way back, he stopped at one of the Coffin Houses and got the food he claimed he'd gone after before he returned to the hideout. Once he was back and his mission was over, he got a chance to take a deep breath and think about what he'd done. He felt as though he'd avenged Brian's death and got a good start at getting even for what the soldiers had done.

He didn't tell anyone that he went after the soldiers because that was something he would try and keep to himself. He didn't want the girls to freak out about it, and he didn't want to try to explain to Thomas or Aron why he didn't take them with him. He knew he couldn't justify why he felt compelled. He had to do it alone.

Thomas approached him and said, "Hey Cameron, did you see what was happening with the soldiers? We heard gunfire and laser weapons fired, and we were worried about you being out there alone."

Cameron just said, "Yeah, I heard it too. I tried to stay away from them."

He knew Thomas would be pissed at him for going after the soldiers alone if he told him the truth.

He prayed and thanked God for keeping him safe while on his mission. He didn't know how many soldiers he'd killed or wounded but figured it was probably a stupid and impulsive thing he'd done. His actions had now put the entire group in jeopardy, and he felt frustrated that they would have to leave their hiding place as quickly as possible. He knew the soldiers would be actively searching for him and wouldn't stop until they found the guy who attacked their camp and killed their soldiers. He would have to convince everyone that they had to leave the hideout.

***

Chapter 7

When everyone was up, Cameron pulled them together and said, "After we killed those soldiers last night, we'll have the rest of the soldiers searching for us all over this place. We've also been getting a lot of activity lately, and I believe more soldiers are moving into this area. They seem to be coming in from the west coast and moving east, just like my dad said. I think it's just a matter of time before they find and kill us. He thought, "If everyone knew what I did to the soldiers this morning, they'd be angry with me and in a hurry to get out of here, too." He continued, "We don't need to hide out here and wait for that to happen. We need to get out of here as soon as possible. Let's pack our things and leave as soon as possible."

I think we only have two choices where we should go. We can return to the cabin and hang out until all the ice melts and this war is over, but it may only be a matter of time before the soldiers find us up there. The other option is to travel to the Area 51 secret military base in Nevada and find the entrance like the American soldier from the hotel told us we could do. Maybe we can stay ahead of the enemy soldiers and not get killed. Once there, we can give the secret password and see if we can get in. If we can get inside, we can seek the help and protection of the military inside the underground base."

Rachel was the practical thinking person of the group and said, "Cameron, you do know that the Area 51 secret military base is built in the middle of a dried-up lakebed called Groom Lake? What if we get there, and the Base is under the ice and filled with water? It will melt even faster in the desert because it's at least 10 degrees warmer than here. We might also have trouble finding the entrance. What will we do if we can't find it or get in?" Cameron replied, "That lakebed has been dried up for a long time, and if we can't find the entrance or if it's underwater, then we'll try to find Area 52, which isn't too far from Area 51. Getting there on these snowmobiles may take several days, but it's our best option. If they're both covered in water, we'll head east toward the Denver Airport and find the entrance to the underground base.

Maybe somewhere along the way, we might get lucky enough to run into a few more American soldiers or armed civilians like ourselves that we can join up. I don't feel uncomfortable about going back up to the cabin and just waiting for the soldiers to find us or having to fight with survivors to keep our food. I'd rather be doing something other than being like sitting ducks. We'd be just like target practice for the Russians. I know that I don't want myself or any of you to be skinned alive, like what they did to Brian."

That stung Thomas like a knife when he said that. He was still angry about the way the soldiers had killed Brian.

During their meeting, everyone agreed that if they stayed under the overpass, it was just a matter of time before they were found by the soldiers and killed. The decision was made to pack everything and head east to Area 51 and see what the United States military had planned for all the survivors.

They quickly began loading everything up and got ready to leave. The group filled their snowmobiles with gas and checked the oil before leaving. Cameron said, "Let's take what we can carry on the snowmobiles and leave the rest here. Thomas, you strap a shovel to your snowmobile, and I'll strap one on ours, and we'll carry the rope with us." Once ready, Cameron said, "Let's take the 85-mile drive south to Bakersfield and head east on the route 58 path that cuts through the mountains. It's the lowest mountain pass road, and getting to the Mojave Desert and toward our destination is much easier. Once we get to Mojave town, we can take route 14 north until we reach Highway 178, which will take us east and deeper into the desert. I've heard the area 51 base is about a hundred miles northwest of Las Vegas."

Staci told Cameron, "From now on, Cam, I want to be right by your side no matter what may happen to us. I don't want to be left alone again. It scared me this morning when you were out getting food alone, and we heard all the fighting going on." He told her he felt the same way about her and assured her he was good with what she said.

Before they left, they gathered together and prayed for their families and Brian. As they headed south toward Bakersfield, Cameron, and Staci took the lead on their snowmobile, Rachel and Aron behind them, and Thomas brought up the rear. It took about 5 hours, and a few bathrooms stopped until they reached the bottom of the hill just east of Bakersfield.

When they arrived, they could see activity on the path, with footprints and vehicle tracks heading in the direction they were going. Cameron had the group pull over for a minute as they examined the tracks and talked about what they saw. Cameron said, "It's hard to tell if these tracks are from survivors or soldiers. It's just hard to know for sure. They might be from soldiers because there are a few ATVs and snowmobile tracks. You can't tell which direction they took in this ice, but there's only one way to go unless we go off the path."

They talked for a few minutes about their options. Cameron asked everyone if they wanted to continue east on the route or take another one that didn't look like there had been any activity. He said, "If we take another route, it may be treacherous and unforgiving. We may be facing a lot of unforeseen obstacles along that way. We could fall into one of those deep crevasses and not be able to get out alive."

Thomas said, "We must keep going on this route and take our chances. If we run into some of the soldiers, we can try to avoid them or stand our ground and fight, whichever we do."

Aron and Rachel shook their heads in agreement.

As they headed east and higher into the mountains, it became a steeper climb as the elevation started changing dramatically. They were just over the highest crest of the mountains and on their way down when they came to a large rounding curve. Just as they were rounding the bend, they were ambushed by a squad of soldiers that hit them with heavy small-arms fire. The soldiers were hidden behind a large ice bank and not accessible for Cameron's group to see until they were fired at them.

The bullets began to fly all around them, and the gunfire hit Aron in the middle of the chest. He is instantly knocked off the snowmobile from the impact of the bullet. Although Rachel was riding behind him, she wasn't hit and tumbled off the snowmobile.

She quickly crawled over to Aron and tried to get a response from him, but he was choking for his last breath. She screamed out in heartfelt pain when she realized he was dying. Seeing there was nothing she could do for him and bullets were zinging all around her, she scrambled for cover behind an ice mound not far away. The rest of the group jumped off their snowmobiles and covered behind an ice mound. The soldier was about 50 yards out and behind an ice mound about five feet high and forty feet long. It was directly in front of them and on the bend of the curve. They couldn't go forward or back words and were trapped.

The soldiers were spread out behind the ice bank and firing over the top of it toward Cameron's group. Cameron yelled to Thomas, "It looks like a squad of eight to ten of them. Hold your fire, and let's figure something out. We can't do anything while they're hiding behind that ice. Let's wait for the soldiers out and see if we can get them to move toward us. Maybe they'll think we aren't armed and send a few advancing soldiers over the ice toward us, and then we'll pick off a few of them." After receiving fire for several minutes and not getting anything in return, the soldiers stopped firing in their direction. Cameron yelled to Rachel to see how Aron was doing, and she told him that Aron was dead. Cameron screamed out, "Those sorry pieces of crap, I'm sorry, Rachel." She didn't respond to Cameron as she just sobbed.

Cameron told everyone to hold their position and not get too anxious. He said, "We're in a waiting game with the soldiers." It had been about thirty minutes after all firing stopped when the Russians did what Cameron thought they would do and sent two soldiers over the mound of ice. They were crouched over at the waist and moving toward Cameron's group. They were like a creeping Tiger after its prey. Cameron whispered, "Hold your fire until they get a little closer. I'll give you the signal when to fire." When the soldiers got within 30 yards of them, Cameron took careful aim and told Thomas, "You take the one on the right, and I'll take the one on the left. Fire on them once I count to three." Once Cameron said three, the two soldiers were instantly hit and went down. A volley of bullets came again from the remaining soldiers behind the ice mounds. Cameron yelled out to hold their fire, and the group held their fire and waited for Cameron to give them further instructions.

After several minutes, the firing from the soldiers went silent once again. Cameron said, "Let's wait until it gets a little darker, and then I'm going to sneak around to the left side of that ice mound and see if I can get in behind them. Thomas, you see if you can move around to the right side and come up behind them from that side. Once we get in behind them, then let's take them out. They won't have any place to go as we pick them off individually. Give me at least 20 minutes to get into position. Staci, you, and Rachel stay here and remove any of them that start coming over that mound of ice toward you. In about 15 minutes of fire, just a couple of rounds in their direction to distract them."

It was a slow process of staying low and low, crawling to finally make sure the Russians didn't see them get around behind them. One soldier stood guard at the rear of the rest of them, watching for anyone coming up behind them. It was just a few minutes after they were in position when Rachel and Staci fired a few rounds each toward the soldier's position. As soon as they did, Cameron shot an arrow deep into the middle of the lone guard's chest. Cameron instantly loaded his bow and fired another into him to be sure he was dead.

Thomas was in a firing position between two blocks of ice and took careful aim. Several soldiers left that had their weapons over the top of the mound of ice, and once they received the incoming rounds from Rachel and Staci, they began returning fire. They never expected anyone to sneak up behind them because they had their guard. As soon as Cameron killed the guard, Thomas waited just a few minutes, and then his automatic weapon sounded out with a loud burst of shots toward the soldiers. His initial volley instantly took out a few of them, and Cameron did the same from the other side with his automatic rifle. Now, the Russians were trapped with nowhere to go instead of the other way around.

Thomas and Cameron continued to take them out as the remaining soldiers tried to find a place to take cover. Not having anywhere to hide, two remaining soldiers jumped over the huge mound of ice toward Staci and Rachel. Staci and Rachel opened fire upon them when they came over the ice. They were able to hit one of them, and the other took off, running toward a large block of ice about 30 yards away. Cameron saw the soldier running for cover, so he took careful aim and shot him in the middle of the back. Once he went down, Cameron shot him a couple more times to make sure he was dead. Thomas carefully approached the dead or dying soldiers and put a few extra bullets in each of them.

Once the firefight was over, Rachel was able to rush to Aron's side and broke down in sobs. Aron and Rachel had been together for several years, and she was devastated by his death. Rachel had spent every minute with Aron, and during this entire survival ordeal, they looked out for and protected each other.

After letting her have time alone with him for several minutes, Cameron went over to her and gently asked her what she wanted to do with Aron's body. She said, "Can we please tie him on the back of my snowmobile and take him with us until we find a place to leave him? Maybe we can find a good spot up the mountain and pray for him before we leave him there. I don't want any of the soldiers mutilating his body as they did, Brian."

Cameron replied, "Yes, we can do that, Rachel. I'm sorry. He was a great guy and meant a lot to all of us. He will be greatly missed, but we must leave here as soon as possible because it's getting dark." As they left, he and Thomas quickly secured Aron's body to the back of Rachel's snowmobile.

Thomas noticed the 5-gallon gas can tied to the back of his snowmobile had a bullet hole, and about half the gas was gone. They untied the gas can and poured the remainder into Cameron and Thomas's snowmobile. Cameron told Rachel they would take Aron's body until her snowmobile ran out of gas. If they were out of harm's way from soldiers, they would leave the snowmobile and his body there and have a short service for him.

Rachel was distraught and still crying as they left the scene of the ambush. Cameron was concerned about her driving the snowmobile by herself because she was all over the path as she wiped away the streaming tears running down her face. Cameron had her follow behind him and Staci since it was getting dark. If Rachel could follow them, it would make it easier for her. Since she insisted that she carry Aron's body on the snowmobile, they had no choice except to let her do things the way she wanted.

Seeing that she had a hard time, Cameron pulled up beside her and asked her if she would be ok. She couldn't speak but assured him she was by moving her head up and down. Cameron wasn't feeling good about letting her go alone, so he said, "Hey Rachel, why don't you ride with Staci, and I'll take your snowmobile and Aron."

Rachel replied, "No, thank you, Cameron, but I want to do this myself. I have to do this for Aron, and I need this time alone with him if it's ok."

Cameron replied, "Ok, Rachel, whatever you want to do, I'm just worried about you, that's all." She thanked Cameron for his concern and said, "I'll be ok."

They were soon back on the path again and heading toward the desert. The group got about 10 miles up the canyon, and the cliffs were on the right side of the trail. It was a 200, and 300 feet drop to the bottom. If you were to make the wrong turn or weren't paying attention, it meant instant death once you went over the dark edge of the cliff. After passing a few of those spots, something strange happened to Rachel. When they came out of one of the turns and next to one of the cliffs, Rachel's snowmobile shot past Cameron and Staci with her hand on the gas at full throttle.

As she passed them by, she yelled out, "I love you guys, I'm sorry." She headed over the cliff and disappeared into the dark canyon below. They could hear her last scream on the way to the bottom.

Staci also screamed, "No," the entire time.

Cameron and Thomas immediately pulled up and shut off the snowmobiles and quickly jumped off. They ran over to the cliff's edge and looked down. The snowmobile burst into flames on impact, and they could see the crumbled and shattered bodies of Rachel and Aron lying at the bottom and close to the burning snowmobile. Staci had her hands over her eyes as she temporarily took them away and looked down. Once she realized Rachel was dead, she turned around and wrapped her arms around Cameron's neck and sobbed.

She kept saying aloud, "Why would she do something like that? That was crazy."

Thomas shook his head and said, "Man, I never expected her to do anything like that." I guess she couldn't cope with losing Aron. It must have just been too much for her." The three took several minutes and said a few prayers for Aron and Rachel before returning to the snowmobiles and dredging forward.

As they headed to Mojave's small, iced town, Cameron wondered if their group would survive what lay in store. There were now only 3 out of the original six that were still alive. Staci looked exhausted and still shaken by what Rachel had done when she suggested to Cameron that they find a place to hide out for the rest of the night.

***

Chapter 8

Around midnight, the three reached Mojave's small town, 58 miles east of Bakersfield, at 2762 feet. When they first arrived in the frozen little town, everything was covered in Ice, just like the San Joaquin Valley. Almost all houses had collapsed under the weight of the heavy ice, and only a few chimneys sporadically rose into the sky. When they looked across the ice, it was hard to tell where the houses stood. There were only indentions in the ice where the roads had been.

Unfortunately, none of the mobile homes in the United States survived the storm, including the town of Mojave. The mobile home couldn't support the ice's weight. They also weren't equipped with fireplaces, and only a few owners had generators.

When Cameron was younger and passing through Mojave during the summer, he wondered why anyone would want to live there. He thought it was so hot you could hardly breathe at a temperature of around triple-digit degrees heat.

They searched, found an empty building, and headed to the main floor. They used their battery-operated heaters to keep themselves warm until morning. After another restless night, they were up early and began to look around for survivors.

Cameron said, "We need to see if there are any survivors in this town, but it doesn't look good. I don't see any activity."

"Maybe everyone is dead," replied Staci.

They began to drive slowly down what looked like the ice streets, searching for any signs of life. They descended the road until they spotted a young boy about fifty yards away. He quickly darted in front of them and down into a hole in the ice. For a brief moment, it reminded Thomas of one of the ground squirrels out on the ranch that ran for cover once you got close to it. They drove their snowmobiles to where they had seen the boy disappear and parked. They walked over to the hole in the ice and started shouting hello and hoping to get a response. They could tell the area had been used frequently because the ice was packed around the opening.

It took several minutes until an older man in his seventies came slowly up the ice opening. He had a rifle in his hands, and it was aimed at Cameron's chest. Everyone quickly raised their hands as Cameron whispered to Thomas and Staci, "Oh man, not this again. "He quickly told the old man, "Hey, Mr., we're not looking for any trouble. We're just passing through and trying to see if a few people in this town survived that crazy storm and if we can get some gas for our snowmobiles."

The older man had an entire head of gray hair, gray mustache, and beard, and he was looking down the barrel of his rifle with one eye squinted and his mouth closed stiff and firm. His clothes looked like he had been wearing them for a few weeks without washing them. He still wasn't saying anything and might pull the trigger at any moment. Feeling uncomfortable, Cameron said again, "Look, Mr., we're not looking for any food or anything like that; we have our own. We're from Fresno, and we survived the storm while on a ski trip and staying in a Cabin in the mountains. There were six of us, but we lost two members around Tehachapi when the Russian soldiers ambushed us. We're just hoping we could find some gas for our snowmobiles, and then we'll be on our way to Area 51 to meet up with American soldiers in the underground base. We've been fighting Russian soldiers for the past month or so and trying to keep from being killed."

Cameron gave him a little more information than maybe he needed, but he was trying to gain the man's trust. It took a few minutes before the old man seemed to relax as he asked, "So what you're saying is that Russia has something to do with that storm and all this crap we've been going through?"

Cameron replied, "Yes, Sir, they're the ones that brought this storm down on us with some weather warfare program, and they are invading

America right now with their ground soldiers from the East and West coast."

He lowered his weapon and shook his head as he continued, "Those S.O.B. s, I told my wife Russia or China had something to do with this, but she didn't believe me. We've never had a weather system hit us like this one in my 76 years. They killed almost all our friends and neighbors with that damn storm."

Cameron shook his head and said, "You're not the only ones. That storm killed most of the people in California and the United States. We heard from an American Soldier we met in Fresno that only about 20% of the American population survived. Unfortunately, the Russian Soldiers are now going around and killing all the survivors they can find."

Cameron introduced everyone and said, "As I said, we've lost three of our close friends who also survived with us. They were with us until the past few days. One was killed when he was skinned alive by the Russians. We hid under an overpass in Fresno and went out at night to get food. One of our friends was killed yesterday while on our way here. His girlfriend was so distraught that she drove her snowmobile over one of the cliffs to her death."

The old man now had the rife lowered and by his left side as he replied, "Man, I'm sorry, that sucks. My name is Charlie Snow, and my wife, daughter, and two Grandsons are here with me. It was one of our Grandson that you saw and followed to our location. He glared as he said, "He wasn't supposed to be outside the shelter, and I'm not very happy with him right now."

Cameron said, "The fact that the Russian Soldiers are heading your way, I can certainly understand your anger with him, Sir. The soldiers aren't interested in taking prisoners, and they seem to be hell-bent on killing every survivor they can. They don't care if it's a man, woman, or child. They'll kill all of you if they find you here."

When Cameron said that, Charlie got angry and said, "Yeah, well, let them come. We'll blow them away."

Cameron thought, "This guy is living in his little world and has no idea what the Russians will do to his family."

Thinking that he was blowing off steam, Staci changed the subject and said, "So, how did you and your family survive the huge storm? Not very many families were as lucky as you."

His demeanor suddenly changed, and he smiled and motioned for them to follow him as he proudly said, "Come on down, and I'll show you."

Cameron and Thomas removed the snowmobile's keys and stuck them in their pockets. They looked around to ensure no one was watching them and entered the large hole in the ice.

When they reached the bottom of the entrance, Thomas said, "Hey, Charlie, is this what I think it is?

Charlie looked back with pride as he puffed out his chest and replied, "Well, if you guessed it's a nuclear bomb shelter from the 1960s, you would be right."

Thomas shook his head up and down and said, "Yep, that's what I thought it was he looked around and said, "Nice," as he stepped into the shelter.

As soon as they made their way inside, a gray-haired woman in her late sixties to early seventies and a middle-aged brown-haired woman stood shyly beside her. The two Grandsons, around ten or eleven years old, stood directly before them. The women nervously had their hands on the boy's shoulders. Cameron introduced the three and reviewed the same story he had told Charlie.

He told them this was his wife, Millie, and she quickly said, "This is our daughter Catherine and our two grandsons, Luke and Max. Charlie looked over at Max with an angry look on his face and said, "We're lucky these people are friendly, or they may have killed all of us. I'm not happy with you right now, Max."

Millie quickly interrupted Charlie and said, "Would you like to join us for something to eat? We've fixed a stew using canned corn, carrots, potatoes, and tomatoes. It's not much, but you can join us if you'd like."

Staci looked at Cameron and Thomas, and they agreed that it would be good to relax for a while and enjoy something other than what they had been eating for a few months.

Once they had stewed, they could talk about the bomb shelter and what it was doing there. Charlie was pleased to talk about it as he told them that when the fear of the Cuban missile crisis was over, he could pick up the bomb shelter cheaply. He said he and his sons dug out a hole right next to the house and put the bomb shelter in place. They cut out a door on the bomb shelter and the side of the house. They put hinges on it and then put it back on the shelter and sealed it.

Once the snow had gotten high, Charlie had his family stay in the shelter for fear that the house might collapse. He had it stocked with about a month of water and several months of survival food. They still had access to the three-bedroom home and bathrooms even though the roof had partially caved into the house. They were fortunate the top didn't collapse to the bottom of the house. The toilets wouldn't automatically flush but would flush if hot water was poured into them. The flush handle had to be held down at the same time. Charlie told them he wasn't sure how long that would last.

By the time they got through eating, it was starting to get dark, and Millie knew they had a long way to go, so she asked them if they wanted to stay for the night before they continued to their destination. She said they could stay in one of the bedrooms that hadn't collapsed.

Before they went to sleep for the night, Cameron told Charlie that the Russians were advancing toward them and would be there within a few days. He told Charlie they had killed a squad of them on the way from Bakersfield. He told Charlie the soldiers would search for them after what they had done.

Cameron asked Charlie and Millie if they wanted their family to accompany them to Area 51 so they could be safe.

Charlie said, "Nah, but thank you, son. We're going to stay here and take our chances. When those Russians come to our door, we'll lock ourselves in the shelter, and they'll have to blow us up to get to us."

Cameron replied, "You know, Charlie, they might just do that, but if you keep quiet when they try to get in the bomb shelter, they may never know you are there and give up on trying to get in after a few days." Cameron thought it was a crazy idea, but it might be their only chance of survival if they weren't willing to leave.

Charlie said, "I'm glad you kids showed up and told us what was happening; now we'll be prepared to handle the Russians when they arrive. I know you didn't see them, but about four to five hundred people survived the storm and hid in different locations. We have some under the several overpasses on Highway 58, and others are hiding in the old silver mines in the mountain just south of town off Silver Queen Road."

Thomas said, "You got to be kidding me; we didn't see anybody before we spotted your grandson."

Charlie replied, "That's what I'm talking about; these people know how to hide." As soon as you guys leave, I'm going to get together with the townspeople and let them know the Russians are heading our way and that they'll be here soon. Everyone will be prepared to give them a hell of a fight. We'll arm ourselves and protect our families. We ain't let them take away what little we have left. We got our pride, you know, and ain't no Russians that can take that away from us."

Cameron said, "I admire your attitude, and we wish you a lot of luck with that, but if your people survive the attack from the Russians, you'll have to move somewhere once the melting ice floods everything around here."

Charlie frowned and replied, "Yeah, we've thought about that, and once the water starts seeping in, we'll move to higher grounds. We can take shelter in the mountains not far from here. There are train trail caves that cut through the mountains, and it's perfect for us to stay protected. We've already moved food, water, and weapons, so we've been preparing to go there. We can hold off a big group of Russians if they come after us. Once the water runs us out, we'll get the rest of the survivors and move up to the caves."

Thomas replied, "That's awesome, Charlie. Sounds like you've got a plan and have it all figured out. You're one bad dude."

Charlie smiled and beamed with pride.

All three were mentally and physically drained from fighting with the soldiers and losing Brian, Rachel, and Aron the past few days, so they quickly welcomed the hospitality. It was going to be the first time they slept without a lot of fear in a few months.

The following day, Charlie wakes Cameron and Thomas early and tells them he knows where they can get a gas can and drains a gas tank to get enough gas to reach their destination. He had a good friend who didn't survive the storm with a gas can and a pick-up truck. They could punch a hole in the gas tank and get what they needed.

Once they were outside Charlie's home, Charlie's armed friends surrounded them. Charlie had gotten up early and told his friends about the Russian invasion. He told them that the soldiers were heading in their direction.

He told Cameron they would get gas for the two snowmobiles from his friend Norm's house. He told the men to spread the word that they needed to meet with all the survivors to decide what they would do before the soldiers arrived. He told them that after Cameron's group left, they would figure out what they would do." As Charlie turned to leave, the men quickly left to tell other survivors what they had found out.

On the way to get the gas, Charlie tells Cameron and Thomas that Norm is his best friend and that he hasn't made it through the storm.

He said he tried to get him to come in with them before the storm got bad, but Norm chose to go it alone.

Cameron replied, "I'm sorry; he was a good guy."

Charlie just smiled and looked down as he said, "Yeah, he was a good old boy. We were friends for over fifty years." After they got the gas can and gas, they went back to Charlie's hideout.

Once back, they filled the snowmobiles and strapped the gas can to Thomas's snowmobile. They then went inside the shelter and thanked Millie and Catherine for the food and hospitality. They shook hands with Luke and Max and said goodbye. They thanked everyone before they packed everything up and were ready to go.

Staci hugged Millie and Catherine as she wished them luck before returning to the top of the ice.

"Millie yelled to them, "You kids take care of yourselves, and good luck to you too."

Cameron and Thomas shook hands with Charlie and thanked him for everything. They also wished him luck before they boarded the snowmobiles. He told them they didn't need to worry about them; he said they'd been surviving out there in that little town their entire lives, and there were no Russians that were going to ruin it for them now. He said, "We'll be just fine. My friends and I'll fight them for their money if they come looking for trouble around here."

Cameron laughed and replied, "You know something, Charlie, I think you will. Kill a bunch of them for us while you're at it."

As they got back on track and headed north, Cameron thought, "This is what America is all about. These poor people didn't have much of anything except for a small house and a (bomb shelter), but they accepted the three of us like we were long-lost family members. They took us in, fed us, and let us stay the night with their family without knowing much about us." He thought it was heart-warming and comforting. It was sad that many people like them had not survived the storm.

When they finally stopped for a few minutes to get their direction, Cameron said, "I sure hope those poor people survive whatever the Russian soldiers might try to do to them, but I'm not sure they'll make it."

Staci and Thomas shook their heads and replied, "Yeah, it's so sad because I like that family, and they were so nice. She was a little sad as she said," Reminded me of family."

She had tears as she said, "I miss Rachel."

Their next stop was Ridgecrest, which was approximately 60 miles north.

***

Chapter 9

As they made their way north, they noticed occasional smoke coming from homes buried in the ice with just chimneys sticking upward. They decided not to stop at any of the houses or would never reach their destination. However, they were happy to see that other people had come through the storm as they gave each other the thumbs up each time they saw the smoke drifting slowly into the sky. The stories of survival were fascinating, but a few of the stories were hair-raising and amazing. Cameron thought, "It's mind-blowing how resilient human beings can be when looking at death directly in the face."

It took them about four hours to get to Ridgecrest, and once there, they were able to find a few survivors of the town and started asking them questions. While talking to the locals, Cameron told them they were trying to make it to the area 51 secret military base and unite with the base's underground soldiers. One of the survivors suggested they go about two miles east on Highway 178, and they would run into the China Lake Naval Air Station. The locals said they had military personnel stationed there to inform them where it was located and how to get there. He said they had a military guard stationed in front of the base the last time he visited the facility. Cameron thanked him for his help, and they immediately headed the few miles to the Base.

When they arrived at the base, two American military guards dressed in uniforms had staked out an area on the highway's north side. It appeared they were directing a few survivors to a different location. They parked their snowmobiles and made their way over to one of the soldiers, and when they were close enough, Cameron gave him a salute, and the soldier returned it. Cameron asked if they could talk briefly and ask questions regarding area 51. He smiled and told them he would try to answer any questions they might have but didn't know much about that base.

Cameron told the soldier that he had been a Captain in the U.S. Army and had served six years of active duty before recently leaving the military. He briefly went over what they had been going through since they survived the storm. He told the soldier they had run into an American soldier in Fresno who was the sole survivor of a firefight with the Russians. The Fresno soldier said they could seek refuge at area 51 if they could make it there.

The soldier listened intently to what Cameron had to say and then said, "Area 51 is about 200 miles north/east of here, and it will take you at least three to four days to get there on those snowmobiles. You can try it, but you'll need a reason to get in once you're there. They won't take in all survivors that show up there and try to get in."

Cameron asked him if they couldn't get into Area 51 or 52. What did he think about going to the Denver, Colorado, underground base and trying to get in there? The soldier said, "I don't think that will work, Sir. There is already so much water rushing down the Colorado River the banks are overflowing. Seven states drain their excess water into the Colorado River: Colorado, Arizona, Wyoming, Utah, California, and Nevada. It won't be long before nothing can cross that rushing water. It's also a matter of time before the Lake Mead Dam collapses, and all hell will break loose in Las Vegas and surrounding areas. Everyone who survived the storm must find caves and other places in the higher mountain ranges to keep from being under all the water.

In this area, the entire desert is just huge dried-up lake beds and valleys, and they're all going to fill up with water as soon as all this ice melts. It could reach several feet deep and maybe up to 20 or 30 feet in some areas. The water will also take a long time to absorb, drain, or evaporate. It won't be long before we lock things up here and vacate the base. We're concerned about how the survivors left around here will make it with very little food and not much shelter. Even in higher elevations, it will get interesting when winter returns. We're afraid people will start killing each other for food and other survival items.

We have the same problem with the Mississippi River; a massive flood will separate the United States into three sections until the water is gone. There will be land east of the Mississippi River, west of the Colorado River, and between the two rivers. The entire United States could be underwater except for the higher mountain areas."

Cameron replied, "Yeah, we've already thought about that. We have the same problem with the San Joaquin Valley in California; it's already getting water and will fill up like a fishbowl. All the invading soldiers must retreat to the coast-line mountain region or go up into the Sierra Nevada mountains. The soldiers and survivors will be trapped in those higher areas, and it could be a hell of a mess. Our troops are now trying to mount a counteroffensive that will soon be heading west to intercept the advancing Russians, but they will have the same problems with rising water as the Russians and survivors. We hadn't thought about the rushing Colorado River; that could be a problem for us crossing it if area 51 doesn't work."

Cameron asked the soldier the last question as if there was a place they could stay for the night while trying to figure out what they would do. He told them about a shelter in the middle of the town that had been one of the hotels set up temporarily as a safe house. He gave them directions to get there, and Cameron thanked the soldier for his information and saluted him before they left.

They followed the soldier's directions and soon found the shelter. It was a three-story hotel, and the ice went to the bottom of the third floor. They parked the snowmobiles out front, took the keys, and went inside. A few older women welcomed them and showed them rooms with several empty cots in each room. There were sleeping bags and thick, warm blankets stacked on each cot. A few survivors were hanging out on a couple of the cots and talking to each other. The women told them they could pick out any cot, making themselves welcome while staying there. She told them they had food and water in one of the empty rooms if they wanted to help themselves. They thanked the woman and then went over to the corner of one of the rooms, picked out a cot for each of them, and put their things on them. They went to the room with the food and water and got a few things to drink before they tried to relax and figure out their route to Area 51.

Even though it was comfortable there, they still had a restless night of sleep and were up early and ready to go. When they got ready to leave, they went to the entry and looked outside to see if the snowmobiles were ok. They were surprised to see there was already a group of five younger survivor men who had weapons in their hands, and they were checking out the two snowmobiles. They looked like they were figuring out how to start them without the keys. When the three saw the men checking out the snowmobiles, Cameron motioned for Staci and Thomas to duck behind a wall and pull their rifles from their shoulders. They quickly stuck a clip in the rifle chamber when Cameron went over to them and whispered, "I'm going to go outside and confront these guys and see if I can convince them to back away from our snowmobiles. Thomas, you, and Staci each go around and come up behind them while I'm talking to them and have their attention. If they don't back off and try to get tough with me, I'll let them know you have rifles pointed at them."

Thomas said, "You got it, Cameron. Give us just a few minutes to get in place before you go out to confront them."

When they were ready, Cameron had his rifle drawn when he walked outside to face the group. He said, "Is there something I can help you guys with?"

One of the young men who acted like he was the group leader replied, "Yeah, man, we like your ride. We've been talking it over, and we're going to take them, so if you have the keys, you need to give them to us."

Cameron said, "I'm sorry guys, I can't do that; those belong to my friends and me." A few of the guys had their weapons drawn and aimed at Cameron as the leader continued.

"If you don't give us the keys, then we're going to kill you and take them from you."

Cameron said, "Just like that? Are you guys willing to kill me to take our snowmobiles? That seems pretty screwed up to me."

The guys were laughing and waving their guns around, and the leader said, "Yeah, man, it may be screwed up, but that's the way it is, so you just need to give us the keys."

Cameron laughed and said, "Well, I'm not going to give you the keys because those snowmobiles belong to my friends who have guns pointed at you and are ready to kill you if you don't back off and me."

Cameron pointed to Staci and Thomas, who were behind them, and had their rifles pointed at them, and said, "They are ready to kill several of you on my command." When he said that, the men looked around and saw Staci and Thomas with their rifles pointed at them.

Cameron said sternly and severely, "I don't think those snowmobiles are worth all you guys dying for, do you? Not waiting for an answer, he continued, "I would suggest you move away from them right now and throw your guns over that ice embankment over there," He pointed to the location he was saying. "I would do it, guys, because none of us want to play games with you. We've already killed many people to get here, and killing the five of you wouldn't hurt our feelings at all. Do you understand what I'm telling you?"

In Cameron's voice and demeanor, the young leader could tell that he was serious as he took another look around at Staci and Thomas.

He said, "Ok, man, take it easy. You're right; none of us needs to die for those damn things. We're good." Even though his words sounded surrendering, he wasn't moving away from the snowmobiles like Cameron had asked. Cameron could tell these guys didn't want to give up on the snowmobiles without a fight.

Seeing their reluctance to move, Cameron said, "Drop your guns now, over the ice mound as I told you, and move about thirty yards in that direction while we get on our snowmobiles and get out of here. Thomas, if they don't move away from them within the next ten seconds, then kill the guy doing all the talking. Staci, you kill one of the other ones. I don't care which one. Pick out the one you want to kill first. It doesn't matter which one."

Thomas replied, "You got it, Cameron. It would be my pleasure to take him out."

Staci gripped her rifle tighter and said, "I'm ready when you are, Cameron. Just give me the word; this could be fun."

Cameron started to count from ten backward, and the young man finally realized Cameron's group wouldn't ask them again. The leader raised his hands and told the other guys to do what Cameron demanded: drop their guns and move away.

He said to Cameron, "Ok, man, you win. We don't want to die for them."

After doing what they were told, Cameron told Thomas and Staci, "Get on your snowmobile and start it up, and I'll cover you while you do. After they were safely on the snowmobile, he had Staci and Thomas keep their weapons aimed at the guys until he could get on his snowmobile and start it up. Once they were safely on, they sped away from the group of men who were now scurrying for their guns and shouting and cursing at them as they drove off.

They drove about 5 miles east of town, pulled over, and Cameron had Staci jump on the back of his snowmobile.

She said, "That was a little scary. I didn't think those guys would back off for a few minutes. We might have to kill a few of them to get them to back off. From now on, we've got to be a little more careful where we leave the snowmobiles. It was just like Jerry told us; those idiots were willing to kill us for our snowmobiles."

Cameron replied, "Yeah, I didn't expect them to be so aggressive, but thank you for backing me up. We got lucky and dodged a bullet; it could've gotten nasty." They then headed north/east toward their destination.

It took about four days to find area 51, and when they got there, they were intercepted by a group of American soldiers who had their weapons drawn and aimed at the three of them. They were told to follow the soldiers to the entrance of the base. A couple of soldiers' squads were gathered outside the base entrance talking. Cameron thought they looked as though they were getting ready to go out on a mission because they had backpacks, weapons, and all the standard equipment of a military infantry company.

Once at the entrance, a company Lieutenant approached them and said, "Who are you guys, and what are you doing out here?" Cameron explained that they had run into a sole survivor from Area 51 who told them they could find safety at the underground base. He told the Lieutenant they had come from Fresno and told him about his military history.

After telling their story to the Lieutenant for several minutes, he said, "Bring your snowmobiles down, and we'll put them inside in a safe location for you. I want to take you guys to meet with the General; I'd like him to hear your story. Cameron thought it was weird that he wanted them to talk to the General because that doesn't usually happen, but he told the Lieutenant they would meet him. The Lieutenant told them to wait a few minutes while he talked to the General alone for a few minutes.

The Lieutenant returned after spending several minutes with the General and immediately took the three to meet up with four-star General Jack Thompson. General Thompson was in a room about fifty yards from the entrance and approximately 20 feet by 24 feet. It was impressive as it was equipped with computers and a lot of other communication equipment. A few Army technicians were working at nearby desks. There was a blackboard on one wall with a lot of scribbling. General Thompson was sitting at a large desk with several phones in front of him. He was getting off the phone when they were told to come in.

The Lieutenant was able to introduce them to General Thompson. He was an older man around his mid to late fifties with a typical crew haircut and graying temples. Cameron stood at attention as they were being introduced and saluted General Thompson.

In a deep, stern voice, he returned the salute and said, "So, Lieutenant Jenkins here was telling me your story of survival. Are you from Fresno, California?"

Lieutenant Jenkins spoke up and said, "This is Cameron. He was a captain in the Army for six years and was recently honorably discharged. He spent two tours of duty in Afghanistan and oversaw a combat infantry unit. We could use his and their help since we were talking this morning about sending troops to that area in Fresno. You said you wished we knew more about the area. His friends are Thomas and Staci, and they survived the storm together."

The general said, "Why don't the three of you take some time, get a nice hot shower, food, and water, and relax? I want to talk to you later when I have more time. How would you feel if we all could get together after dinner?

Cameron said, "That would be great, Sir. Just let us know when and where." He saluted General Thompson and turned and followed Lieutenant Jenkins to a room with cots and blankets. He pointed to a wall closet and told them there were towels for them. He showed them where the hot showers were located and then told them he would come and get them for dinner in a few hours. He left them and went about his business.

It wasn't home, but the three of them welcomed the idea of taking a hot shower and getting food and a good night's sleep without having to worry about the Russian Soldiers trying to kill them. It was the first time they didn't have to worry about the Russians killing them in a few months.

After a full-cooked dinner, Lieutenant Jenkins took them to meet with General Thompson again. He was much more relaxed and did not talk as sternly as earlier. As they sat and listened intently to what he had to say, he went into an extended and complete breakdown of the United States Strategy and their plans to stop the Russian invasion. He told them they were regrouping troops all over American to intercept and engage the enemy soldiers and either drive them out or kill them.

He looked at Cameron and said, "We're not familiar with the Central Valley of California, and we understand there's a large regiment of Russian soldiers in that area. We have reason to believe they have set up a headquarters in Fresno. We need help in locating them."

Cameron said, "Yes, sir, it looks like they have an entire battalion of troops in the center of an old town, Fresno. We've already had some confrontations with them and killed a lot of their soldiers in that area."

General Thompson said I need to ask a huge favor from the three of you, "I know this is a huge request, but would you be willing to go back to that area to help us find their location? You guys could save us a lot of time and troop lives. I can send a couple of radiomen with you so they can keep in touch with us here at headquarters and let us know their exact location and everything we need to know about the Russian soldiers. Once we know their location, we'll send our troops to take them out?"

Cameron wasn't expecting to hear anything like that. The three of them were hoping to find safety in the underground base. They hoped to stay with the soldiers until things were back to normal. Now, General Thompson asked them to return to where they'd just come from to locate the enemy soldiers and report their location to him. Cameron thought the entire idea was just bizarre. They had spent the last few months hiding from the Russian soldiers to keep from being killed, and now they were being asked to go looking for them. Cameron told General Thompson they would have to talk to each other alone and see what they thought about returning to Fresno.

General Thompson said, "Why don't you sleep on it and tell me your answer in the morning."

Cameron said, "That would be a good idea because it's something all three of us have to agree on." They saluted each other, and then the three of them went back to their room.

That night, they sat on the cots and talked about what General Thompson was asking of them. Staci said, "I can't believe the General wants us to return to that place. I don't think he realizes how dangerous and hard it is out there hiding from the Russians and trying to stay alive."

Cameron said, "Yeah, that's a lot to ask of us, especially after we've already lost 3 of our original group because of the enemy soldiers. As they continued to talk, Cameron said, "I don't think I can sit here every day and do nothing after the General has asked us for our help. Every day I was here, I would feel guilty for not doing my part to stop the Russians. It's not just about helping the General, it's about helping America and our troops. I feel like I owe it to our friends who died and our families, so I would be ok with going back, but it would be up to the two of you to make the final decision."

Thomas said, "I don't feel at home here. I'm like you, Cameron. I don't want to bury my head in the sand and wonder what's happening. Especially if the General thinks we can be of some help to our country. I don't have a problem going back. I'm still angry with what the Russians did to my family, Brian, Aron, and Rachel."

Staci said, "Ok, I will do whatever you two want. It's hard to turn the General down when he was so sincere and needed our help."

Cameron replied, "If we all agree, then we'll tell him in the morning that we'll go back. It's not going to be an easy thing to do; it is pure hell out there."

The following day, the three met up with Lieutenant Jenkins, and General Thompson and Cameron told him they had decided to return to Fresno and help find the Russian headquarters. He told the General that he would like an extra radio tuned to the right frequency so he could also communicate directly with the base if something happened to the soldiers he sent with them. He also wanted enough food supplies to return to the Fresno area for several days. General Thompson knew Cameron was right and agreed with his request. They attached the extra radio to the back of Cameron's snowmobile. They gave him the information on contacting the base headquarters as they loaded up snowmobiles with supplies and were getting ready to go. Lieutenant Jenkins assigned Specialist E-4 Russell Ferguson and Specialist E-3 Bruce Miller as radiographers who would be traveling with them. The two of them would be on Army all-terrain vehicles and not snowmobiles.

Once Ferguson and Miller were ready to go, the three thanked General Thompson for his hospitality and told him they would do their best to stay in touch with him once they spotted the enemy. They decided to take a different route back to Fresno instead of the way they had come. They would go through the mountain path through Walker Pass. The mountains in that area weren't as high as they are further north in the Sierra Nevada, so it would make traveling a little easier.

***

Chapter 10

It took about four hours to make it through the mountain path of Walker Pass before they started to see what once was wide-open meadows, but now everything was covered with ice. There were tops of houses and ranch barns scattered a few miles apart throughout the area, but there weren't any signs of human activity.

It was time for them to stop, take a break, and try to get something to eat when they spotted a lone weak flume of smoke drifting up toward the sky. It came from the chimney of a small rooftop. The house was off to their left and very near the base of one of the nearby mountains. Cameron thought the place looked dangerously close to a massive overhang of ice that appeared to be about to break loose from the hill and come down at any time on the poor inhabitants of the house. Without even stopping, Cameron motioned for everyone to head in that direction.

When they got close to the house, they could see just the fireplace chimney sticking out of the ice, and someone had dug a pathway down to the front door.

Specialist Ferguson said, "You guys let me, and Miller checks it out, but keep an eye out for enemy soldiers." Ferguson and Miller pulled out their rifle and approached the house opening.

When they got closer, Ferguson said, "Hey guys, come look at this." Walking over to the top of the opening of the ice, they saw patches of blood in the ice, like something or someone had been hurt or killed and lost a tremendous amount of blood. Ferguson and Miller had their weapons pointed toward the opening as Ferguson started yelling out to whoever was inside.

After a few minutes, an attractive but frazzled-looking young girl who looked in her early to mid-twenties came slowly out of the front door. She was about five feet, three inches tall, and had light brown hair, long and stringy. She appeared attractive but looked like she may have been through some tough times since the storm hit. She was holding a rifle awkwardly under her armpit and aimed in the direction of the group.

Ferguson said, "Hey, you need to put that gun down! We have our rifles aimed at you, and if you don't put it down, we'll blow you away."

Ferguson said to Miller, "Hold your fire. It doesn't look like she knows what she's doing because she's not handling that rifle correctly."

She said, "Ok, but please don't kill me; I don't have much food to give you." She put the gun down to her side and stood looking up at the two soldiers.

Ferguson said, "We're not here to rob you or take your food. We saw your smoke and thought we'd check on the people inside. You could be in danger here with that Ice above your house.

She replied, "If you don't want my food, what do you want?"

By then, Cameron was next to Ferguson and Miller and said to her, "We saw the smoke coming out of your chimney and wanted to see how many survivors were here because that mountain of ice above your house looks like it could come down on you at any time. When that happens, your entire home could be covered in hundreds of feet of ice."

Realizing they were concerned about her well-being, she noticed everyone was the same age. After talking for a few minutes and feeling comfortable with them, she asked them if they wanted to come down inside.

Cameron told Specialist Ferguson and Miller he, Staci, and Thomas would go inside and talk to her if he was okay with that.

Ferguson said, "Yeah, you guys go on down and find out what's going on with her and all that blood, and we'll hang out here and keep our eyes open for Russian soldiers. We'll let you know if we have any problems up here."

Cameron replied, "We won't be here long, but keep your eyes open. There's a lot of blood outside this place, but we need to find out what happened." They could see more splatters of blood almost to the front door on the way down into the house.

Once inside, the girl offered them a place to sit. She began to tell them what had happened to her husband and why there was so much blood outside. They could tell she was still struggling with what happened as she began to tell her story. She said her name was Kirstin, and her husband was Vince. Her husband was a Veterinarian, and they had bought the little horse ranch three years earlier, right after he started his practice. They thought it was the perfect place because it was away from the large cities. She said her husband kept them alive during the massive storm by burning wood constantly and spending all their time cuddled together by the fire.

Fearing that she might have killed him, Staci slowly spoke up and asked, "So what happened to him?"

Kirstin broke down, put her face in her hands, and cried uncontrollably for a few minutes before saying anything. Through the tears and sobs, she finally said, "He died a few days earlier when he went out to get more wood from the woodpile." A family of Mountain Lions live in the caves up there in the mountains. Vince sometimes had to shoot his guns in the air to keep them away from a few heads of cattle we own. Vince said he saw the mother with two younger ones about six months ago. I told him he needed to shoot them, but he didn't feel right about killing them because he believed in saving animal lives.

They must've waited for him when Vince went out to get the wood. The larger female and one of the more giant female cubs attacked him and had him down before I realized what had happened. By the time I got the rifle loaded and to the front door, they had already killed him. I'm not very good with a gun, but I started shooting at them. I fired about four shots, but I don't think I hit either of them. It was already too late for Vince because the large female had his neck in her jaws, and they were dragging him up the ice. They weren't afraid of the gunshots and continued to pull him away even while I was shooting at them.

They must've been starving to be that brave. Seeing that he was dead and there was nothing I could do for him, I turned and ran back inside the house and locked the door behind me. As brave as they were, I was afraid they might turn on me and come after me next.

I've been crying for the last two days because I didn't know what to do. I'm almost out of wood and afraid to go outside and bring in more. I've been feeling like I'm trapped and just waiting for the Mountain Lions to kill me, or maybe I would freeze to death once the fire dies down. Vince took care of everything for us. I've always been a city girl and didn't have much experience with country life."

Staci said, "That's just crazy! Not only do we have to fight the Russians, but now we have to worry about the wild animals that survived the storm."

Kirstin looked surprised. She looked up at Staci and said, "What are you saying? What does Russia have to do with any of this?"

Staci replied, "It looks like they are the ones that attacked America with this huge storm. They used some weather warfare system, and they had soldiers that moved in and went around killing all the survivors. We've been hiding from them for the past few months. We've had some battles with them, but our options for hiding are getting harder to find. We've already lost three of the six of the original members that survived the storm with us,"

Cameron said, "Yeah, we ran into an Army soldier in Fresno who told us we'd be safe at Area 51, so we went to the underground military base and met up with a General. He wanted us to go back to Fresno and find the Russian headquarters they had set up there. That's one reason we have the two Army soldiers with us: we're heading back to that area. Once we locate the Russians, those guys will call the General and give him the Russian location and how many soldiers they have. He can send in troops to take them out. "

After that, we returned to the cabin in Shaver Lake, where we had survived the storm. We believe the Cabin may be one of our safest options. We were safe there but wanted to find out about family members, so we left the safety of it and searched for our loved ones. We went to Fresno and then to Ivanhoe and found my family and Thomas's family all dead."

Kirstin said, "I'm sorry for your losses."

Staci said, "We're sorry for your loss too."

Cameron was getting a little anxious, so he said, "You need to come with us because if you stay here, you'll eventually die one way or the other. If the Mountain Lions don't get you, that ice is coming down on you, and you'll never dig your way out. If not, you'll freeze to death." Thomas told her she could ride on the back of his snowmobile if she wanted to come with them.

They told her they probably had some rough areas to go through before they got to Fresno or the Cabin but didn't have much choice. She told them she had no reason to stay there but didn't want to burden them.

Cameron said, "You won't be a burden. We're not going to leave you here to die. Get ready and put on an extra layer of your warmest clothes and a heavy coat. Don't take more than a small bag; we have little room for anything else on the snowmobile."

While she was getting herself, Kirstin told them to help themselves with anything they would like to eat and whatever they wanted to take with them. Cameron took a few sandwiches to Ferguson and Miller, and everyone took a few minutes to have a quick lunch. He told the two of them they would take the girl with them because they didn't want to leave her there alone to die.

Ferguson said, "Whatever you want to do, Captain, we're here to back you up." By the time they were through eating, Kirstin was ready to go. She had put on a little makeup, combed back her hair, and put a baseball cap over it. She didn't look quite as messy as she had before.

When they left the house, and at the top of the ice, Kirstin said a few Vince prayers before they left. She said, "If we're going to go through the mountains. If the ice is melting, as you guys say, the river down the canyon will make it impossible to get through. Let's take the first road at the bottom of the hill that Y's off to the right. It's road 107 and a better route past Kernville and through the mountains to the central valley. It will take us upward along the river until it levels out at the top of the steep mountains. Maybe we can reach the top before dark and stay at one of the Ponderosa Lodge cabins. Vince and I stayed there one weekend." Everyone agreed that sounded like a plan as they returned to the snowmobiles and ATVs and headed in that direction.

Cameron was in the lead and followed Kirsten's directions as they took the road path, which followed it around and up past Kernville. Specialists Ferguson and Miller were bringing up the rear. Lake Isabela was to the left of their way and had already reached near capacity. The ice was breaking off and falling into the lake. Kirstin was right, and they wouldn't have been able to take the route past Lake Isabella down the canyon. The river down through the canyon to Bakersfield would have been impassable.

As they followed the river and road path up the canyon toward Pine Mountain, it started getting steeper and more treacherous. They could hear the massive water flow as it rushed under the ice below them. They hoped the ice would hold as they drove the snowmobiles and ATVs up through the rugged path.

After traveling for a few hours, they came to the steepest part of the path before making it to the top and open area. They were having trouble getting to the top, so Cameron hit the accelerator and had it at almost full throttle as he made his way up the river path toward the top. Thomas saw what Cameron had done and decided to do the same as he gunned the throttle. Specialist Ferguson and Miller followed suit a few yards behind Thomas and Kirstin. Just as Thomas reached the middle of the steep path, a massive chunk of ice they crossed broke off and tumbled to the monstrous rushing water below. A large hole opened in the ice. Thomas and Kirstin's snowmobile was riding shot across to the other side of the hole as Thomas and Kirstin tumbled off. Specialist Ferguson and his ATV fell down the big gaping hole into the rushing water below. Specialist Millet was able to turn his ATV to the right immediately and went around the gaping hole.

Staci heard Kirstin's screams and quickly looked back and saw what had happened. She immediately screamed for Cameron to stop. He went about another five more yards until he felt safe for them and pulled up and turned off the snowmobile.

Staci screamed, "Oh, no, the ice broke off, and they went down." All Cameron could think was that the rushing water had swept them away. Thomas was his best friend, and now he feared he'd lost him too. For a moment, he had a sick feeling in his stomach. Looking back, he saw that Ferguson had also tumbled down the hole, but Specialist Miller had managed to dodge it and was safe.

When he thought they would never see Thomas or Kirstin again, they heard their muffled screams. Miller joined Cameron and Staci as they carefully crept up and around to where the ice had split off and fallen into the rushing water below. As they looked down miraculously, Thomas and Kirsten had landed on a flat piece of ice on top of a large rock. It was about three feet thick and about the size of a small car. They were clinging to the ledge about twelve feet from the top of the ice. It was another thirty feet down to the rushing water below. There was no sign of Ferguson or his ATV. Kirstin was hanging onto Thomas like a baby monkey hanging onto its mother.

Cameron laid down on the ice's edge and had his head and arms over the edge, talking to Thomas. After finding out they were alive, he spoke to Thomas about what they should do. The rushing water below was so noisy that they had to yell at each other.

Thomas yelled to him, "If you use the rope, it might cause the rest of this ice to come tumbling down on us, so get the shovel off my snowmobile and dig a stairway down to us. You'll have to do it slow and easy because this entire layer of ice looks like it could give way at any time and take us with it."

Cameron let out a giant lung full of air as he wondered if there was a possibility something like that would work. Thinking about it for a few seconds, he realized it was their only option. He yelled down to Thomas he'd try it but told them to be careful not to slip off the ice because it would take a while to reach them. Cameron told them he would throw him the rope so that they could tie it around them, and then Miller would tie the other end to a nearby tree just in case the plan didn't work. Thomas gave Cameron the thumbs up just before he ran to get the shovel and rope.

Thomas's snowmobile was still running, but it was safe, so Cameron quickly turned it off and grabbed the shovel. He and Staci talked about the best side to approach them and the one where they felt they wouldn't be putting so much stress on the massive layer of ice sitting over a huge gaping hole in the ice. Once they decided where to dig, Cameron started digging about ten feet away and throwing the ice down the hill as he went. He cut an area in the snow about two feet wide and big enough to get them out. He carefully made steps about twelve to fourteen inches apart, leading down to them.

He took his time and worked his way down very slowly and carefully. He was praying the ice would hold until he could reach them. Staci kept a close eye on the ice to see if he caused any cracks as he dug. Because it was slow and tedious, it took Cameron a few hours to finally punch a hole near where Thomas and Kirstin were hanging onto each other. Once close enough, he hadn't even finished the last step when he reached out, grabbed Kirsten around her wrist with his hand, and pulled her up.

He then did the same for Thomas as he came up right behind her. He said, "Thanks, Cameron. I thought we were goners!"

Once they were safe, Miller untied the rope, put it back on Cameron's snowmobile, and put the shovel back on Thomas's snowmobile. It was a narrow escape, but they were back in a safe position.

Thomas laughed nervously and joked, "Man, that was a heck of a way for Kirstin and me to get to know each other."

Once they were safe, everyone hugged each other, and Cameron said, "Hey, man. I thought I lost you. Don't ever do that to me again. That took about ten years off my life."

Thomas smiled and hit him on the shoulder as he replied, "Thank God you guys were all there for us, Bro."

After retrieving Thomas's snowmobile, they boarded them as everyone headed to Ponderosa Lodge again. Once they got to the top of the ice, the mountain flattened out, and they were able to make good time in that part of the mountains. They were able to make it to Ponderosa lodge just before dark. Before going inside, Cameron had Miller call on the radio to inform General Thompson what happened to specialist Ferguson.

When they arrived at the lodge, all five were physically and mentally exhausted as they pulled the snowmobiles and ATV up, parked them, and stuck the keys in their pocket. They cautiously approached the lodge and found a few other welcoming survivors taking warmth inside. After the typical introductions, everyone exchanged their stories, which took a while. The survivors didn't realize what had happened with the storm and that the Russians were killing people. They listened intently to what Cameron was telling them. After hearing what was going on with the Russians, they were now afraid for their safety.

Cameron said, "You need to keep a guard out for them because if they find you here, they'll kill all of you. You might want to start thinking about a place where you can hide when they come looking for you."

After talking for a while, the survivors could tell that the five of them were tired, and they were offered food before being shown where they could stay for the night. Cameron asked if they had a place where they could park the snowmobiles and ATVs so they wouldn't be seen so quickly. One of the survivors took Cameron, Thomas, and Miller outside and showed them where to park them. After eating, they said good night to the survivors and found their place to sleep. They said a prayer for Ferguson before they got some much-needed sleep.

***

Chapter 11

Early the following day, they headed out of the mountains and took the highway 190 path two miles up the road from the Ponderosa Lodge. When they reached the fork in the road, they left and headed toward Porterville. It took several hours to pass a few small towns of Posey, Springville, and then to Success Lake. When they came to the lake, it was already over capacity, and water and slushy ice poured over the Dam. Cameron pointed it out to Miller as they continued down the road path past the spillway. The river below the dam had already reached capacity and overflowed its banks. Above the river, the ice had already dropped down into the river and turned into slow-moving, slushy ice water. It wasn't going to be long before the dam would burst.

They kept traveling westward until they came to the small town of Porterville on the west side of the Sierra Nevada foothills. The city is twenty-three miles south/east of Visalia and sixty-three miles south/east of Fresno. It's mostly a farming community with a lower medium income for the average family. It was around 4:00 in the afternoon when they got to the town. They decided to take a break and rest for a while. They grabbed a bite and went to the bathroom.

They were in the middle of their meal when they heard what sounded like a heavy firefight between two groups, and it was about a mile from their location. Thomas told everyone, "I've been here to Porterville many times, and they have a few two and three-story buildings in the heart of the town. The gunfire sounds like it's coming from that part of town." At first, the group was reluctant to get involved with the firefight because they thought it might be locals fighting over food.

As they listened, the firefight sounded like both sides were using some automatic weapons. Miller looked over at Cameron and said, "That sounds like it may be Russian weapons. I want to check it out and see who's fighting each other. If the locals are fighting over food, we won't get involved, but if they're fighting the Russians, I want to see if I can help them."

Cameron told Miller they tried to avoid the Russians as much as possible and felt that maybe they shouldn't get involved.

Miller said he needed to check it out and find out if the Russians had made it to that area, and if they had, he needed to let the General know.

After talking it over for a few minutes, Cameron, Staci, and Thomas agreed they would go with him and check it out. They got back in their vehicles and headed toward the fighting. When they got close enough, they could tell it was about ten to twelve Russian soldiers fighting a group of local survivors. The Russians had six or seven survivors pinned down at the end of an iced-end road and were throwing a lot of firepower at them. The survivors had been chased or driven into the dead-end street and hid behind several ice mounds. A few dead people on both sides were lying on the ice where the fighting was taking place. Even though they were outnumbered and in a difficult situation, and the locals wouldn't give up easily, they still had some ammunition left and were fighting for their lives.

As they got closer, Cameron said, "We need to help these guys out, or the Russians are going to kill them, or none of them will get out of there alive. He told Miller, why don't we come up behind the Russian soldiers and start taking them out one by one?" It's how they had been doing it in other fights and having great success.

Miller agreed.

Cameron told Miller, Staci, and Thomas to spread out about twenty feet apart across the back of soldiers and behind some ice mounds. He said, "We'll have them in a difficult situation like they have these poor suckers right now. When we get into position, wait for me to whistle, and then we'll start firing on them. Kirstin, you stay with the snowmobiles and shoot anyone that tries to come near them." He figured she could at least scare people away even if she couldn't hit them with a bullet.

The four crept low and stayed out of sight until they could make their way around behind the Russians. Once they were in position, Cameron gave the signal, and they opened fire on the surprised Russian soldiers. At first, the soldiers didn't realize what was happening to them, but soon they started losing their fighters. Then they realized they had been attacked from the rear and started scrambling to find a place to hide and return fire. They were trapped and caught in the crossfire from the local group in front of them and Cameron's group behind them.

Now, the Russians were the ones fighting to survive. They couldn't go toward the survivors, and they couldn't back out toward Cameron's group. They were now being picked off individually, just like Cameron had hoped. They continued to fire on the soldiers until all of them were either dead or wounded. After the fighting was over, Cameron looked over at Staci, Thomas, and Miller, and that's when he realized Miller had been hit by one of the soldier's bullets. Once all the soldiers were killed, Cameron raised his weapon in the air from the mound of Ice to let the survivors know it was safe for them to come out. As the survivors slowly exited their hiding places, they yelled and cheered because they knew they had been saved from certain death. Cameron quickly ran over to Miller, and unfortunately, he was dead.

Thomas had also taken a bullet and was bleeding from his left shoulder. Cameron ran to his aid and asked him if he was ok.

Thomas raised his weapon in the air with his right arm and replied," Yeah, I think the bullet bounced off my left shoulder bone, but it's bleeding like crazy. It's more superficial than anything; I need to try and stop the bleeding and get a wrap and pressure on it." Staci came running up to check things out, and that's when Cameron told her Miller was dead and asked her if she would take Thomas to the snowmobile. They had an emergency kit with bandages and tape on one of them. She and

Thomas headed for the snowmobiles as Cameron waited to talk to the survivors.

At about that same time, the survival group leader came bounding up to Cameron, and he was excited as he wrapped his arms around him and said, "Hey Dude, that was badass. Thanks for saving our lives. We were done for before you guys came in and saved us."

Cameron replied, "Hey, I'm glad we could help you guys out. My name is Cameron, and the wounded guy there is Thomas, and that's Staci with him. I hope you didn't lose too many of your friends."

The young guy lowered his head and said, "Yeah, we lost a few of our close friends, but it could've been all of us if it hadn't been for you guys. My name is Nicko Martinez."

Before the survivors joined him, they checked on their fallen comrades and then took the rifles and ammunition from the dead soldiers. Cameron was surprised to see that all the survivors were young people in their mid to late teens, and even Nicko wasn't much older, maybe eighteen to twenty. Cameron asked him how they got into that predicament, and he said, "The market is right below that area where we've been getting a lot of our food for the last few months, and the Russians must've been staking it out and waiting for us. They trapped us, and we were done for before you got here."

Nicko told Cameron that a few of his family and friends had survived the huge storm. They had now taken refuge in a large cave deep in the side of the mountain, only a few miles from there. He told Cameron they originally had about 25 survivors, but they lost two more today, and we're now down to about 16. You guys must return to the cave and meet my dad, our group leader. We have a nurse at the cave who can help your friend with that wound."

Cameron replied, "That may not be a bad idea. Thomas needs to have that shoulder wound checked out."

Cameron told Nicko to take the two Russian all-terrain vehicles and the four snowmobiles that the Russians were riding and load up their dead friends' bodies, and take them back to the cave with them. He told Nicko they would load Miller's body on his ATV and follow them back to the shelter. Before he loaded Miller's body, he said Nicko. His group would have to stay away from this place from now on because he believed the Russians would be searching for their group after they killed their comrades."

Cameron went over and told Thomas that Niko's group had a nurse back at their cave, and maybe he needed her to look at the shoulder wound and get it stitched up. After Niko's group was loaded and ready to go, they had Cameron's group follow them to their hideout. Before now, the locals had been walking everywhere they went because they had no all-terrain vehicles or snowmobiles to ride. Taking the Russian equipment was going to be very helpful to their group.

When they got to the cave, they were met by several middle-aged men and women holding automatic weapons. Niko rode ahead of the group and told his dad it was ok. He told his dad that the people with him had saved their lives. Once they were off the snowmobile, one of the older women in the cave came out, got Thomas, and took him inside to treat his wound while Niko introduced his three new friends to his dad and the rest of the group.

The lady treating Thomas was soon beginning to stitch him up. She didn't have any numbing agent but poured Tequila over the wound as she stitched him. Thomas winched in pain and let out a few yells every time she ran the needle through his skin. When she was done, he asked her if he could hold Tequila's bottle and took a massive gulp from it as he said. "Damn, I don't think those stitches hurt as much as that shot of Tequila I received."

While Thomas was being stitched up, Cameron, Staci, and Nicko took Miller's body, along with the body of Niko's friends, to an area a short distance away, where some of the other members in Nick's group had been laid to rest. Cameron took Miller's dog tags off him, and he and Staci said a prayer over him as they covered his body with ice.

Cameron gave the dog tags to Nicko and told him to hang on to them until the General's men met up with his group and then gave them to the soldiers.

They then returned to the cave and met with Manuel Martinez's leader. He was about five feet seven inches tall with a stocky build. He had thick black hair and a thick mustache. Niko was sad as he told Cameron his mom hadn't survived the storm. Manuel was a farm labor contractor and had overseen a large group of Mexican laborers working in the fields, picking oranges, grapes, and other crops. He was used to being in charge, so the group of survivors had no problems overseeing their group.

Manuel asked Cameron if he and his group would like to stay the night and let Thomas's wound feel better before continuing to where they were going. Staci and Kirstin were starting to get to know the group's women, so they thought staying the night was a good idea. It was already getting late in the day, and they would've had to find a place to stay soon anyway. It was going to work out perfectly for them.

Cameron got on the radio with the Area 51 Base headquarters and let General Thompson's men know they encountered Russian Soldiers in the small town of Porterville. He told them his group and some locals had killed 12 enemy soldiers, but Miller was killed during the firefight. He told him he hadn't seen a headquarters for the Russians, but the ones they killed seemed to be a squad of a larger group. He gave General Thompson's men the location of the town of Porterville so that they could send soldiers to that location.

Cameron told Manuel that United States soldiers would be coming to Porterville from Area 51 to help them out against the Russians. He didn't know how long it would take for them to arrive. He told them they'd have to protect themselves from the Russian soldiers. He told Manuel he would show Nicko and some other young men how to use the laser weapons on the Russian ATVs and snowmobiles.

Manuel brought out the Tequila and began passing it around. Cameron's group enjoyed the hospitality and indulged in a few shots of each firewater. They laughed and had fun with Manuel's group before they could cuddle up close to the fire and stay warm for the night.

The following day, Cameron kept his promise to Nicko and showed him and his friends how to use the laser weapons before they packed up things and got ready to leave.

He told Niko, "We're going to leave you Miller's ATV, which you can give to the American Soldiers when they come to help you. Try not to take the same route back here to the cave each time you return from getting food, or the Russians will figure it out and come after you. You have enough firepower now with all these laser weapons and other weapons to kill a lot of them if they do come after you."

Niko thanked him again for saving their lives and said, "Good Luck out there, my friend."

They shook hands and thanked Manuel for letting them stay the night and for the hospitality before they got on their snowmobiles.

Manuel said, "Thanks for saving my people. We are thankful to you, and good luck on your journey."

After they were back on the snowmobiles, Thomas laughed and said he couldn't tell which was worse, the pain in his shoulder or the headache he had from the Tequila he had the night before. He thanked the woman who sewed up his shoulder before they left.

They traveled along the west side of the foothills on their way back to Fresno. When they got close to the small town of Exeter, Thomas pulled up next to Cameron and said, "We're only a few miles from my family ranches. I want to stop there, and maybe we can pick up some additional supplies."

Cameron gave him a thumbs up and told him that would be a good idea.

While they were sitting there talking, they realized that someone had been following them. They could hear the faint sounds of another snowmobile coming up behind them.

Cameron said, "I'm going to leave Staci here with you and Kirstin, circle, and come up behind whoever is following us. You guys find a place to stay hidden just in case it's someone trying to kill us. He then headed in the opposite direction and circled behind the lone person on their trail.

When the snowmobile got close to where Thomas and the girls were hidden, it pulled up and sat idling. Cameron could tell it was one of the Russian snowmobiles, so he slowed down, pulled his rifle from his shoulder, and took aim at the intruder. His arm was on the rider as he pulled up behind the snowmobile.

The rider immediately put her hands in the air and said, "Don't shoot; I'm one of Niko's friends."

Cameron asked her, "What the hell are you doing following us? You could've easily been killed sneaking up on us like that."

She told Cameron that her brother was one of the guys killed by the Russians in Porterville the day before, and she didn't have any reason to stay with the group in the cave anymore. She told him she wanted to join up with his group. Cameron tried to talk her into returning, but she said she wouldn't.

She said, "Whether you take me in or not, I'm not going back to that cave and waiting for the Russians to find and kill us all. I'm a good shot, and I can help you guys if you have another run-n with the soldiers."

Cameron had her go forward and meet with Thomas and the girls as he drove up next to them.

Cameron said, "She's from the group in Porterville, and her only family member died yesterday in the firefight against the Russians. She wants to join our group and says she will go it alone if we don't let her. She claims she's a good shot and can help us protect our group."

Staci asked, "So, what's your name, girl, and how old are you?"

She told them her name was Karmen Hernandez, and she was sixteen.

Staci looked at Cameron and said, "It's ok with me if you want to let her join us. She has her snowmobile and weapon, and I suppose we can use the extra protection."

Cameron looked over at Thomas, and he shrugged his shoulders as if to say it was ok with him.

Cameron replied, "Ok, we'll let you join our group, but you must carry your weight. There are no free rides here."

She smiled and said, "No worries, I'll help you guys. Thank you!"

***

Chapter 12

When the group got within a mile of Thomas's home ranch, they spotted smoke coming from Thomas's mom and dad's house. Thomas was in denial from the fact that his entire family had all died from the storm. When the reality set in, he got angry because he now believed it might be Russian soldiers taking refuge in the house. He felt the anger rise in his body, and his face flushed as they pulled up a short distance away and stopped. They were about a quarter-mile from the house when Cameron pulled up next to him and said, "Let's be careful here, Thomas. This is either Russian soldiers or some survivors that have taken refuge in the house."

Thomas knew he was right and was angry as he said, "Yeah, you're right. Let's be careful and see if we can draw whoever is out there. If it's Russian soldiers, then let's kill all of them."

When they got closer, their weapons were drawn as they parked the snowmobiles about 100 feet from the house entry. They slowly walked toward the opening, and their guns were aimed toward the door. They were ready for a fight if it was Russians. Cameron had Karmen and Staci cover them from a safe distance, just as if they were soldiers, and they came out firing their weapons.

Thomas started yelling at the people inside, saying this was his house. Whoever was in there needed to come out and show themselves. It took a few minutes, but then Thomas's brother Jason very excitedly came lumbering through the door shouting,

"Thomas, is that you?"

When he first saw Thomas, he went running up as he said, "Man, I thought you were dead."

Cameron quickly told Staci and Karmen it was ok, so they lowered their weapons.

They embraced each other, and Thomas said, "Man, am I glad to see you? I thought you were dead like the rest of our family. Is there anyone else with you?

Jason replied, "No, my roommate, Matt, was with me, but the Russian soldiers killed him while we were on our way back here. Jason saw the dried-up blood on Thomas's shirt and said, "What happened to you?"

"It's no big deal; it's just a flesh wound. I was shot by the Russians when we were in a firefight in Porterville, but we can talk about it later."

Jason told Thomas he'd found the bodies of everyone, and he was angry and depressed about it since he'd gotten there. While Thomas and Jason were catching up with each other, Staci, Karmen, and Cameron moved the snowmobiles up close to the house's opening and went down inside.

Once inside, Thomas introduced Karmen and Kirstin to his brother as they sat down to tell their stories of survival to each other. Jason already knew Cameron and Staci because they had gone to school with Thomas at Cal Poly. They told Jason about their old roommate Brian, Rachel, her boyfriend, Aron, who had been killed, plus the two Army soldiers who died after leaving the cabin's safety up at Shaver Lake.

Thomas asked Jason how he and his roommate Matt had survived the storm, so Jason began telling the entire story.

"Matt and I got a job working at the Walmart Super Store on Higuera Street in San Luis Obispo doing clean-up. We worked after hours, and once the rest of the employees had left for the night. We worked three nights per week until six in the morning.

When the storm first hit, we didn't think much about it because we were busy working and hadn't noticed what was happening outside, except that it hardly ever snowed in San Luis Obispo. When it kept snowing, we realized something weird was going on. At first, we just laughed and then went about our work. We occasionally looked outside, thinking the snow would let up and stop anytime. As you know, it didn't, and it just got heavier.

By the time we got ready to lock up the store in the morning, the snow was already about 2 feet deep outside. When we went out to get to our car, we couldn't because of the deep and heavy snow still coming down. You couldn't see more than a few feet in front of you. Matt and I went back into the store as we watched and wondered how to return to our apartment.

After a while, we realized we needed to ride the storm inside the store. We went to several couches and hung out there for hours, hoping the storm would stop. We were lucky to be in Walmart because we had plenty of sleeping bags, blankets, food, and water inside the store. It started getting cold inside the store, but was not that bad initially. However, the longer the storm lasted, the colder it got.

Walmart had a Mega Hurricane Storm Shelter for sale, and it was on display inside the store. It's six feet high, seven feet long, four feet wide, and supposed to hold six people. It had a vent that we could leave open just enough to make sure we didn't suffocate. Matt and I started throwing sleeping bags and thick blankets into the shelter as it grew colder. We went to the sporting section, and each put on a few layers of long-johns, snow skiing clothes, and insulated after-ski socks and boots. We also got all the lanterns and heaters that ran on batteries and everything else that would keep us warm and threw them in. We went to the aisle where all the water, chips, and food were located and threw an entire box of chips into the shelter. We also stacked several bundles of fake fire logs with us.

Once it stopped snowing, we burned the fake logs inside that shelter for ten days. No matter what we did, it was still cold, especially outside that shelter. We only left the shelter for a few minutes to go to the bathroom or grab something we needed. We were beginning to think the storm may never end until we woke up one day, and the temperature started getting a little warmer.

Once comfortable, we shoveled our way to the top of the ice, returned to the sporting goods section, and got a couple of snowshoes. After we went outside, we slowly returned to our apartment. We didn't see another living being the entire time we returned to our apartment. We were starting to believe we were the only people in San Luis Obispo who survived the storm.

After three weeks of hanging out at the apartment, we heard sporadic gunfire in different parts of San Luis Obispo and realized we weren't alone. When we checked it out, we found that Russian soldiers had moved into the central part of town and soon could tell they were killing people. They weren't asking any questions as some of the survivors tried to surrender. They killed a lot of the people, execution-style, right where they found them. They did take a few alive, but we didn't know what they were doing with them.

When we saw what they were doing, we went back to Walmart and got a couple of high-powered semi-automatic rifles and ammunition to protect ourselves if they found us hiding in the apartment. We weren't going to let them kill us without a fight. Matt's parents lived in Fresno, and mine lived in Ivanhoe, so we decided we weren't going to stay there and let the Russians find us and kill us. We decided to walk back to the valley and see if our families had survived the storm.

We put the rifles over our shoulders, stuffed a small two-person tent, sleeping bags, and food into backpacks, and headed east of San Luis Obispo toward home. We decided to take a direct route north/east over the mountains. It was slow-moving, and we could only go about eight to ten miles daily. We walked during the day and rested for a few hours at night. It took us about four days before we got close to Kettleman City.

During the night of our fourth day, we were camped out in one of the deep crevices in the ice just east of Kettleman. We thought we were safe and protected in that spot, but we weren't. We'd just made ourselves something to eat when we heard vehicles heading toward us.

It sounded like about a half-dozen of them, but there were three or four ATVs and two riders on each one. We immediately scurried for cover behind one of the ice mounds, and the Russian soldiers came up behind us and in front of us, and we were trapped.

As they started getting closer, we started firing at them with our high-powered rifles. We fought for about thirty minutes and were able to kill a few of them before the fighting slowed down. We were stuck, and it was just a matter of time before they killed us. Knowing that we were trapped, I told Matt to follow me as I began to retreat to an area that was a lot darker and had more ice mounds. When Matt started to move in that direction, he was hit in the back by the enemy gunfire. He went down and yelled out that he was hit. I went back to get him, but his wound was so severe that he couldn't get back to his feet. He told me to get out of there and that he wouldn't make it. At first, I told him I wouldn't leave him there, but he told me not to be stupid and to tell his family he loved them once I found them. The soldier's incoming fire had become more intense, so I waited a few minutes and saw that Matt was losing consciousness and wasn't going to make it. I took off running wildly into a dark ravine just below us and away from the gunfire when I slipped into a hole in the ice. It was weird because I didn't go to the bottom. I fell into a hollowed-out area about eight feet below the top of the ice.

I hid in the hole, and the Russians hunted for me for over an hour and couldn't find me. They finally gave up looking. After a few hours, I could sneak out and watch as the soldiers left. I was shivering from the fear and also the cold. After they were gone, I went back to Matt's body and said a prayer for him, got my things and left. I knew I had to get out of there before the soldiers returned. I walked all the rest of that night and saw no other soldiers.

I bypassed the town entirely, ensuring I had no additional encounters with the soldiers. It took me another few weeks to return to the ranch. Since I got here, I've been hanging out and hoping the

Russians didn't come after me and kill me. When I heard your snowmobiles, I thought you were soldiers, and I was done for, so I hid."

Thomas told Jason the entire story about how the six had survived the storm but lost three original members. He told him they were returning to the cabin after they gave General Thompson the soldiers' location in Fresno. He said Jason, the ranch would be under several feet of water because all the dams in the mountains would burst, and the water coming down from the hills would be like huge rivers. He said they would have to get to Fresno and then back to the cabin before that happened. He told Jason he needed to go with them and that they had to leave the ranch behind. Jason told him he was okay with doing that because he knew nothing was left for him there. He also wanted to stay with Thomas. Cameron told him they would go early to get his things ready. He told Jason he could ride on the Snowmobile with Karmen.

The following day, everyone was up early and ready to go. They continued northward until they got close to Fresno. The closer they got, the more activity they saw with the Russians. Cameron pulled over, and they talked about it. They decided they couldn't go any further toward Fresno, fearing they might be caught in an ambush. Cameron called General Thompson, gave him the heads up on the Russians, and gave him their headquarters location. He told him they couldn't get any closer because too many soldiers were there.

Cameron talked to the group, and they decided to go east to route 168, which would take them back to the cabin. Cameron said, "On the way back up there, let's go by and check on Jerry and Ann and let them know what we've found. We can tell them about the ice down in the valley and how the Russians are killing all survivors.

On the way toward Jerry and Ann's house, they noticed large amounts of smoke coming from what they believed to be homes scattered throughout the mountains. It was thick black smoke, unlike the white smoke that gently floated out of chimneys from burning firewood. Cameron pulled everyone up, saying, "This doesn't look good. That's not fireplace smoke."

They continued upward, but as they got closer, they could see something drastically different from Jerry and Ann's house. They slowed the snowmobiles down, and Cameron told everyone to be cautious as they approached. When they were close enough to observe the area, they noticed several dead soldiers still lying outside the house's perimeter. The house had been burned to the ground and was still smoking. It appeared that Jerry and Ann had put up a fight before the Russians burned them out, but there was nothing left of them now.

Cameron quickly turned around and had everyone retreat to a spot down the hill into a tree line area. From there, they regrouped and talked about what they had seen and what they would do.

Cameron said, "That was just bizarre. Those soldiers are just sick individuals."

Thomas said, "Well, now we know the soldiers have already made their way up the mountains. We can't continue to the cabin because they might be waiting for us in another ambush. Even if we make it to the cabin, we would be sitting ducks."

After sitting there a few minutes and talking, Jason suggested, "It looks like the Russians are all around us, so maybe we should head back to San Luis Obispo and take refuge in my apartment. Matt and I were safe there until we decided to leave. Maybe the Russians have already made a sweep through that area and killed most of the survivors, so maybe they wouldn't search the area again. They are moving east, and we may miss them on the way back. We can find another place if they get too close to where we'll be hiding. I know there is someplace on the coastline where we can hide. There must be many empty hotels along the beeches in Pismo Beach."

Cameron said, "That sounds like it may be our best plan, Jason, but how do we keep from getting killed by the Russians while we're trying to get back to San Luis Obispo?"

Jason replied, "We have the snowmobiles, and we can take a more direct route and go straight west over the hills and not take the main road path. We can stay south of Kettleman City because the Russians seem to be following the highway 41 path. If we spot some of them, we can avoid them unless forced to take a stand and fight. If we do have to fight, we may lose a few of our members, but at least we're not going just to wait for them to find us up there in that cabin and kill us. All they would have to do is burn us out at the cabin like they do to everyone else in this area. They'd pick us off one at a time as we came running out of the burning building." After discussing all the pros and cons, everyone agreed they should do as Jason suggested, take their chances, and head west to San Luis Obispo.

Cameron got on the Army radio and called the area 51 base headquarters to let General Thompson's men know what he and his group were doing. He told them there were too many Russian soldiers in Fresno and in the mountain area to stay in any place where they would be safe. He told headquarters the Russians had already infiltrated the Sierra Nevada Mountains and killed all the survivors. It appeared they were sending out their search and destroy missions from the Fresno location to kill everyone. He told him the water was melting fast, and much water was below the ice in the San Joaquin Valley. He said his group's General was heading west toward San Luis Obispo's town near the West Coast.

***

Chapter 13

After regrouping and ensuring they were ready, they headed west toward San Luis Obispo. They had their weapons across their shoulders and were prepared if they had any encounters with Russian Soldiers. They made it about halfway through the first day and were near the tiny town of Shandon when Cameron gave the signal to find a place to set up camp for the night. Many hills were in the area, so they looked for a place off the beaten path hidden from the Russian soldiers' possible route. So far, they had been lucky and hadn't seen any soldiers. Once they had their camp set up, they had something to eat and then decided to get a few hours of sleep for the night. They teamed up and spread out in a half-circle so they weren't all clumped together in one large group, just in case they were attacked while sleeping. They took turns and set up watch duty in case any invading soldiers may find them.

They were up early and ready to continue to their destination with no enemy activity during the night. They traveled for several hours until they reached the mountain's top at Questa Grade, just above San Luis Obispo. Once there, they pulled up and hid in the tree line to see if any Russian soldiers were coming up the grade and had spotted them. While watching for several minutes, they observed a group of about ten soldiers heading in their direction a half-mile down the grade. Cameron told everyone he didn't want to engage them in a fight, so he told them to stay hidden and hold tight. He knew several squads of soldiers usually traveled together as a company.

They pulled the snowmobiles behind thick trees and waited for the soldiers to pass. After they passed, the group continued to wait several more minutes, and they saw another squad on their way up the grade. They continued to hide until several teams of soldiers passed, and no others were heading up the grade. While watching and waiting, it had gotten dark, so they would have to find their way to the apartment in the dark. Once they felt safe, they quickly headed down the grade toward Jason's apartment. It was downhill, so it didn't take long to get to the bottom.

They had Jason lead them to the apartment just about a mile west of the central part of town. Once they arrived, they checked it out to ensure it was empty. Seeing that soldiers or survivors didn't occupy it, Cameron said to everyone, "Once we get comfortable and figure everything out, we can't put any lights on, or the soldiers may see them and come after us. We must find our way around the house by having Jason tell us where everything is located."

Once they were satisfied, it was all clear. The guys went outside and began digging a pathway in the ice down to the garage to park the snowmobiles. They wanted to make sure that the soldiers and none of the survivors saw them just sitting out front because they would have been an instant giveaway to their location. The girls started getting food ready and feeling ok with the place.

That night, they found places in the two-bedroom, two-story apartment where they could comfortably sleep. Even though the Arctic blast was no longer present, it was still freezing in the apartment. It was because of all the ice outside covering a large portion of the apartment. Cameron and Staci shared the same large sleeping bag, while Thomas and Kirstin shared another. They had begun to bond and felt comfortable keeping each other warm. Karmen was a bit of a loner, and everyone thought she had a few demons she was dealing with, so they just let her have her own space. Jason had gotten used to spending time alone ever since he started going to college, so he was ok with being alone.

The sound of gunfire awakened them in the middle of the first night. Jason jumped up wide-eyed, ran to Cameron's room, and said, "That sounds like it's coming from the middle of town, maybe down on Higuera Street."

Staci replied, "Yeah, hearing that gunfire brings back some bad memories and sends shivers up my spine. I hate those sorry pricks."

Cameron pulled Thomas and Jason aside and whispered, "After we get some rest for the night, we'll see if we can find out what's happening. I hope they're not killing college kids who were lucky enough to survive the storm but are now being killed by the soldiers. From the squads we saw coming up Questa Grade and the activity around here, I wouldn't be surprised if those Russians don't have a Headquarters somewhere in town where they carry out all their operations. We'll see if we can find out tomorrow night."

The group relaxed the next day and tried to settle in and feel comfortable with their new home. Most of the people living in the area who survived the storm were college kids at Questa Junior College and Cal Poly University.

Because there were so many Coffin Houses in the area, getting the food they needed was easier. Even though they had gone to college at Cal Poly, the deep ice covering everything made it a little harder to figure out where homes were located. It was still better than being in the mountains, where there weren't many cabins and competing with survivors and soldiers fighting for food. Even with the low survival rate of the survivor, food would soon become a competitive commodity everyone would be willing to fight and die to acquire.

The following night, around midnight, they heard gunfire coming from the central part of town once again. They believed the Russians were killing survivors, and the thought of them killing people angered everyone in the group. As Camron said, "Those soldiers are killing a lot of innocent young people. If that is going on, we can't just sit here and let them keep killing people without doing something about it. They'll eventually find and kill us, too. We need to see where the gunfire is coming from and how many soldiers they have."

Cameron knew whatever they decided. They had to do it on foot; they couldn't take the snowmobiles. He knew if they rode them into town, the Russians would hear them coming and set up ambushes for them.

They had Kirstin stay back at the apartment to ensure everything was secure. Before they left, everyone ensured they had their rifles in their hands with plenty of ammunition and bows and arrows over their shoulders. They split into two teams, with Cameron and Staci together and Karmen, Thomas, and Jason on the other team.

Cameron said, "We're going east to the main part of town, so Thomas, you guys take the street about three streets south to the main part of town. While you're doing that, Staci and I will take highway 1 and head toward town. Remember, we don't want to engage the soldiers right now. We want to find their location and observe what they are doing. We don't want them to know we are armed and ready for them if they engage us."

It took almost an hour, but each team slowly and deliberately made their way through the ice maze until they reached Higuera Street. Once there, Cameron and Staci went south, and Thomas, Jason, and Karmen went north. When they got to the government building between Monterey and Higuera Streets, they met again to talk about what they had seen or heard. There were many lights on the upper floors of the government building and several soldiers walking around inside. Cameron whispered, "look, they have several armed guards in the building. We must sneak out of here carefully so they don't see us. Cameron figured this must be where they set up their headquarters area of operations. It was an ideal building because of its size and location.

They'd only been there a few minutes when they heard the echoing sounds of gunfire from a distance away on Marsh Street. They split up again, and Cameron and Staci took one street east while Thomas, Jason, and Karmen went south to Choro Street and headed east.

When they arrived at the four-level parking garage at the northeast corner of Marsh and Choro Street, it looked as though the prominent soldier's camp was in the structure. They could tell the Russians had tents, awnings, and other things on top of the building, and approximately two hundred men camped in and on the top. It had a

360-degree view of the town and the surrounding streets. The roof was flat, and a ten to twelve-inch thick concrete wall was 4 feet high. The building had an entry on one side and an exit on the other side at the bottom. The soldiers used both exits to go in and out of the structure.

The Russian soldiers were shooting their victims from the top of the building and letting them fall to the hard ice below. Before they killed them, they taunted them by attacking their heads and laughing about it. Cameron's group watched in horror as a few prisoners jumped to their deaths instead of being shot by the soldiers. Staci whispered to Cameron, "Those scumbags are shooting people that look like students, and they're just executing them for the fun of it." Cameron could feel the rage start to build as the blood rushed up to his face, and he said, "Yeah, we have to see if we can do something to stop or slow this down. We can't let them continue to do this every night. We'll have to devise a plan on what we want to do."

After observing them for several minutes, the two teams retreated to a safe distance away. On the way back to the apartment, Cameron found a place under one of the Creek Street overpasses where they could hide if needed. The creek's water was about six feet from the top, rushing down like a river instead of a slow-moving creek. Cameron checked everything and ensured the hiding spot was big enough for them to hide comfortably.

Once they felt safe, they returned to the apartment to talk about what they had seen. Everyone was angry and upset about what the Russians were doing to the survivors. When they went to bed that night, they couldn't sleep well for the rest of the night.

The following day, when they woke, they talked about what they had seen. Cameron had stayed awake most of the night. He had already come up with a plan to retaliate against the Russians. He said, "I think we need to go east to Camp San Luis Obispo Army Base on Highway 1 and get some weapons. It's a training camp and the original home of the California National Guard. We can dig down to the warehouse, where they keep their weapons and other supplies. Let's try to get a huge box of hand grenades and M-16 rifles with ammunition and make sure we have enough to protect ourselves when we go after the Russian Soldiers. I have a pretty good idea where the Wearhouse is located because one of my classes had visited the camp during a school field trip."

Jason said, "That's a great idea. Why don't I take the snowmobile with the laser weapon and be your look-out? If you run into soldiers, I can follow you and Thomas about a quarter-mile behind. Once we're at the training camp, I'll stand guard outside while you guys get everything we need."

Cameron told him that sounded perfect to him.

It was mid-afternoon when they decided to take the snowmobiles and head to Camp San Luis Obispo. It was only about 13 miles away, so getting there didn't take long. Before entering the base, they parked, hid in some trees, and watched for soldiers for about thirty minutes. Not seeing any movement or activity, they headed toward the Wearhouse building where Cameron believed it was.

Once there, they dug down to a door and broke it open. The guys used flashlights and searched the building for hand grenades, M-16 rifles, and ammunition. Finding what they were looking for took about ten minutes, but they could get everything they needed. Jason was starting to get a little nervous as he waited for them. He knew when the enemy was in an area, and you had to get in and out as quickly as possible. Cameron threw a few of the rifles over his shoulders, along with several bandoleros of M-16 rounds of ammunition. Thomas grabbed one side of the grenade box while Cameron took the other side to make it back to the snowmobiles. They joined Jason and strapped the crate of grenades to Thomas's snowmobile.

As they returned to the apartment, two lone Russian soldiers on ATVs spotted them and began to take chase. Jason was hanging around a few hundred yards behind Cameron and Thomas, so when he spotted the soldiers, he decided he would try and take them out. He motioned for Thomas and Cameron to continue down the path as he pulled up at a bend in the trail and hid. When the two soldiers came around the bend, they were only about thirty yards from Jason's position and advancing fast. Jason took careful aim with the laser and took out the lead rider. The other rider tried veering into a half-circle to flee when Jason hit him with a laser beam. He put a few more shots in each of them to make sure they were dead.

Once convinced they were not a threat, he returned to catch up with Thomas and Cameron. They had pulled over a short distance up the path and taken a defensive position in case Jason couldn't take them out. When Jason got closer, he smiled on his face, gave them a thumbs-up, and went past them. They returned the snowmobiles to the apartment and parked them in the garage. Once inside, they asked Jason what happened to the two soldiers.

He smiled and said, "Let's just say there are two fewer Russians we don't have to worry about."

Thomas and Cameron laughed and gave him a high five.

Cameron said, "Ok, guys, we have the grenades and weapons, so now we have to put my plan in place to kill those heartless scumbags without all of us getting killed in the process. Let's get some rest, and we'll go out tomorrow night and place a little fear in the soldier's hearts."

***

Chapter 14

The following day, Cameron told everyone about his plan to attack the soldiers. He told everyone, "We'll hit them about three in the morning with our grenades while they're still sleeping." He took time and slowly went over his plan with everyone, precisely like what he would've done with a squad of his soldiers in Afghanistan. He briefed the guys to ensure they understood their part of the plan. He told Staci she would have to stay with Kirstin and Karmen at the apartment while the guys carried out the attack. He ensured everyone knew what to do before reaching their target. He told them about the hiding area he'd picked out a few days earlier to hide in after the attack. Cameron told them the biggest drawback to his plan was that if the soldiers captured them, they'd probably torture them before they killed them.

Staci wasn't happy about being left behind, but Cameron finally convinced her the three guys had to do this alone. He told her he felt it was too dangerous for the girls to go with them. He tried to ease the tension with her by telling her someone needed to stay behind and protect the other girls, just if the soldiers were to find their hideout.

The night of the attack, they made sure they had their weapons loaded and ready as the guys split up the grenades, so they each had their share. Once Cameron felt prepared, they slowly reached their target on Marsh and Choro street. They inched their way along like tigers stalking their prey. It seemed eerily quiet and creepy that early in the morning, and most of the soldiers were asleep, except for the guards, who were pacing back and forth.

When they arrived at their target, Cameron whispered, "I'm going to run a wire across the exit on the other side of the building and place two grenades on it. When they start coming out of the building, the grenades will blow up and slow down a few of them. Thomas, you do the same thing on the other exit, and then we'll be set. Once you get rid of all your grenades, don't waste time meeting up on the other side of the street."

Cameron whispered to Thomas, "After you have the grenades set in the exit, start counting backward from 10 and then immediately go to your side of the building," Because there was no roof on the flat roof building, the soldiers were fully exposed and venerable targets. They each took a section of the building, and once everyone was in place, they began pulling the pins on the grenades and throwing them up and over the ledges of the four-story building. Each took less than a minute to throw their 12 grenades over the top. They were landing on top of the sleeping soldiers as the grenades found their marks. They started exploding like the 4th of July fireworks. The sleeping soldiers didn't realize a group of survivors was attacking them. Once they had gotten rid of all 36 grenades, the guys immediately regrouped across the street and headed for the hiding place Cameron had picked out earlier under the creek overpass.

As they turned and looked back, they could tell that some of the soldier's ammunition started exploding, and bullets were flying wildly in every direction. There were screams and moans as the soldiers tried to find a place to hide. As secondary explosions continued to go off, they were able to kill a lot of the soldiers.

It took several minutes before the remaining soldiers regrouped and started rushing out of the building on their ATVs. The soldiers in the lead position tripped the wires, and it pulled the pins to the grenades in the exits. The guys were close to their hideout when they heard the four explosions.

Jason smirked as he whispered, "Sounds like we got a few more of them."

It had slowed the soldiers down enough so the guys could make it to the place under the creek overpass without being seen. They had their rifles ready for a fight in case the soldiers found them. The raid was a huge success, but there was no way to know how many soldiers they had killed. By the looks of things, it was a lot.

The entire next day, they could hear the Russians yelling at each other, and all-terrain vehicles were driving throughout the town, searching for the people who had killed their soldiers.

Later that night and after dark, Cameron peaked out of the hideout and decided they would try to make it back to the apartment. As they were heading back, a group of soldiers spotted them and opened fire from about 200 yards away. Cameron had Thomas and Jason assume a low-crawl position on the ice and crawl ahead. He zeroed in on the soldiers, and as Thomas and Jason were making their way to safety, he returned the soldier's fire. He mainly tried to distract and slow them down so the guys could get-away. He quickly emptied four clips of bullets in their direction before he joined up with Thomas and Jason. Once they felt safe, the three of them returned to the apartment. They stayed hidden outside the condo for about thirty minutes to make sure none of the soldiers had followed them back to the apartment before they went inside.

Once inside, they told the girls what they had done and felt proud of killing so many murderous soldiers. Cameron told everyone they would have to be highly vigilant for the next several days because the Russians were not happy and were hunting all over town for the people who had attacked them.

Although the Russians were searching for them, things were quiet in the apartment for several days as the group hid and waited to see if any of the soldiers had arrived. Not getting any enemy activity, the guys were beginning to get a little worried and restless. The soldiers would soon find where they were hiding and thought they should check out other options on where to hide. Cameron talked to everyone about possibly finding another place. He told everyone he wanted to check out a few caves he knew about in the mountains above San Luis Obispo. He said, "I think the guys should check them out because one of those caves might be a great place to hide from the soldiers. I haven't been to the caves in a long time, but I think I know where they're located. I hope all this ice doesn't cover the entrance to them. You girls must stay here because we don't need all of us going out in a large group searching for them." Staci didn't like staying behind, but everyone felt uncomfortable about their hideout's safety and figured they had to do something soon. She welcomed the idea of trying to find another hiding place.

They left early in the morning and went into the foothill area northeast of town. They kept a watchful eye out for enemy soldiers as they went higher and deeper into the mountains. After a few hours of searching, they spotted an opening in one of the foothills above the ice line, about a quarter of a mile away. It looked like a cave opening, and light smoke was drifting out. As they made their way closer, Cameron said, "Ok, guys, someone is staying in the cave, so we've got to be careful because it might be soldiers. If it's soldiers, we'll back off and try to avoid them, but get ready for a fight, just in case."

They slowly made their way to within about 50 meters of the opening when Cameron spotted someone who had a rifle aimed toward them. His head and weapon were the only things visible above a mound of ice outside the cave. Cameron quickly looked around and spotted another guard about thirty feet from the other guard.

Cameron whispered to Jason and Thomas, "Take cover. We have company, and they have their rifles pointed at us." The three of them immediately spread out and hid behind a couple of mounds of ice. As soon as they did that, a voice from one of the men yelled out,

"Don't come any closer, or we'll open fire on you. We have our weapons pointed at you, and you will die if you come any closer."

He didn't seem to have a Russian accent, so Cameron figured he probably wasn't a Russian soldier. Cameron believed he might be a survivor, and he replied, "We're just survivors of the storm and looking for a safe place to hide from the Russian soldiers." The guy said, "How do we know you're not Russian soldiers just here to kill us?"

Cameron said, "If we were Russians, there would be more of us, and we wouldn't already open fire on you.

There's a group of us hiding in an apartment in town. We have killed a lot of soldiers, so they are looking for our hideout now. We graduated from Cal Poly about ten years ago and were on a ski trip to China Peak when the storm hit. We survived in a cabin at Shaver Lake. We've had some of our friends killed by the soldiers during a few firefights with them." The guard slowly said, "So what do you guys want?"

Cameron said, "Maybe we can talk and find your plans." When the guard heard that, he had Cameron stand up to see him as he carefully crawled out of the ice foxhole. He kept his rifle aimed at Cameron as they began to exchange information.

Cameron asked him if they had encounters with enemy soldiers because they killed all the survivors they could find in town. He told Cameron they hadn't seen any soldiers but had heard the gunfire from town since they'd been there. He said they even went down and checked out the killing for themselves a couple of times. They felt there was nothing they could do against the well-armed Russian soldiers. They had run into a few survivors and took them in while in town.

The two guards met up with the three of them, and that's when they found out that several people were living in the cave. Once he felt comfortable with Cameron, the guard told them they had enough food and water stored in the cave to survive for a few months if they had to. They took the three guys into the cave, showed them around, and introduced them to four more young college guys and five young women. The guard told them a few more caves in the area also had college survivors hiding in them. The guard said they all looked out for each other and tried to protect each other.

They exchanged stories of survival, and Cameron told them he'd been an officer in the Army Special Forces for six years. He looked around the cave and told the young man, "You'll be ok if the Russians send a small squad of soldiers after you, but if they send in a platoon of twenty-five or thirty or a company of a couple of hundred soldiers after you then they'll wipe you out. We've had a few run-ins with them, and they have laser weapons, rocket launchers, and other explosives, so they'll use them against your group to get to you. If they can't kill you with their weapons, they'll blow up the opening or burn or smoke you out and then kill you. You may want to set up your guard station about two hundred yards out so you can see them coming and get your group out of the cave before they surround you. You should pass that on to the other cave survivors because once they kill everyone in town, they'll come looking elsewhere for more survivors to kill."

Before leaving, Cameron wished them luck, saying, "You might also want to be careful with the smoke during the day. The soldiers will spot it and come looking for you. It's a dead giveaway that someone is hiding up here. If I were you, I would burn a fire at night and inside the cave where they can't see it."

On the way back to the apartment, Cameron told Thomas and Jason, "I'm glad we checked the caves out, but after looking at the way they're set up in the cave, I don't think I would want to get caught inside one of those. It doesn't give you too many options. There's no place to hide; they must blow up the cave or wait you out. We'll have to think of other options."

Thomas and Jason agreed with Cameron that it wasn't a perfect place for their group to hideout.

***

Chapter 15

It was the middle of the afternoon when they got back to the apartment, and Staci and Karmen were in hysteria. They were screaming that the Russians had taken Kirstin. The girls were still shaking as they told the story of what happened. Staci said, "Karmen and I were upstairs, and Kirstin was downstairs. Two soldiers broke open the door, and as soon as they did that, Kirstin screamed out Russians. Karmen and I knew they had found our apartment, so we grabbed our weapons, went out the sliding glass door, and jumped off the back deck to the ice below. We ran and hid in the trees until we saw them drag her out of the apartment. We followed them until we believed they were taking her to the parking structure, and then we turned around and snuck back here. There was no way we could've opened fire upon them without hitting Kirstin or getting ourselves killed."

Cameron said, "You did the right thing. They would've just killed all three of you if you would've tried something."

Thomas was angry when he heard the news, and the first thing out of his mouth was, "We've got to get her back. We can't let them kill her."

Cameron replied, "Yes, we do, but let's devise a plan before we just go charging in there like Rambo and get ourselves killed."

Thomas was upset as he said, "Yeah, how are we going to do that? Those solders are thick as fleas on that building, and they're already pissed at us."

Cameron said, "We'll figure something out, but after what we did to them last week, they'll be alert for anyone getting near their camp. Let's think about it and see if we can devise some plan to get her back."

A short time later, Cameron said, "Look, guys, during my time in the Special Forces, I had training in hostage rescue. I know how to get her back, but it will be risky. Unfortunately, we don't have much choice because anything we try has a lot of risks involved in it." He didn't want to tell them precisely what he had planned because he knew they would try and talk him out of it. He said, "I want to try to get her tonight in the early morning hours. We need to do it while the soldiers are sleeping. I hope they don't kill her before we get there."

Cameron pulled Thomas aside and whispered, "If they kill me, then you guys get your stuff and get out of here as quickly as possible. We're not going just to sit back and let them kill her, especially if there is a remote chance we can save her."

He went over his plan with Thomas and was wide-eyed as he said, "You're insane. You can't go in there alone? If you try something like that, they'll kill you for sure, especially if they see you're not one of their soldiers."

Cameron replied, "What other choice do we have? They're going to kill her if we don't try something. Besides, I think it's the best idea. Don't worry about me, Thomas. Pray that it'll all work out."

Thomas replied, "Hey Cameron, I don't want anything to happen to you, and your plan seems too risky. I don't think you should do it."

Cameron said, "I believe it's our only chance to save her, Thomas, and I'm willing to take that chance. I need all of you to have your weapons loaded and ready when I implement the plan. Once I locate Kirstin, "I'm going to tie the rope at the top of the building and throw it over the edge. We'll be coming down it, so I want everyone to keep an eye out for us on our way down and be ready to take out any soldiers that try to shoot us."

Thomas said, "That's some scary shit, Cameron. Just make sure you get back down alive."

Cameron said, "Remember, it has to be a team effort. I can't do it alone." He then went over what he wanted the rest of them to do.

They spent the entire day nervous and edgy, and at one-point, Staci said, "Are you sure about this, Cameron? I don't want anything to happen to you; I love you. This plan of yours seems too scary and risky to me; they could kill you."

Cameron knew it was a crazy plan, but he also knew they didn't have any other options if they wanted to get her back before the Russians killed her. He tried to act like it was no big deal, saying, "I've been in a lot scarier predicament than this in Afghanistan, so this will be a piece of cake. Don't worry about me; I'll be ok." He wondered if what he was saying was to try and ease her mind or if he was trying to convince himself he could get out alive.

He always had the soldiers with him in Afghanistan, and they watched out for each other. He knew everything had to work perfectly, or he and Kirstin would be dead. Everyone was quiet in thought as they nervously waited for the night to come. The time seemed to drag by slowly as they waited until the early morning to go out on Cameron's daring rescue attempt.

When it was time, they left the apartment and split up into two teams like before, and the plan was to meet across the street from the parking structure on the south side of Choro Street. They took their time and carefully crept their way to the target. They could see guards pacing the top of the building, looking for any movement below. The group carefully took cover along the dark path where they couldn't be seen. Once they were in place, they waited for Cameron's plan to unfold.

Staci was highly nervous and edgy as she whispered to Thomas, "I don't like this. I hope he doesn't get himself killed."

Thomas grimaced and replied, "Yeah, I know what you mean."

When he arrived, Cameron waited in a dark area just outside the building to see if he could catch a lone soldier about his size returning to the building. Maybe one that was away from the leading group of soldiers so he could kill him. He had to calm himself because the adrenaline had kicked in, and he was nervous and anxious. As he waited for his victim, he could hear his heartbeat and his knees slightly shaking from both fear and excitement.

He'd been waiting for about twenty minutes when a lone soldier was coming into the structure from guard duty he had just left. Cameron looked around to make sure no one was watching as he quickly snuck in behind the sleepy soldier and ran a knife deep into the back of his brain, just below the skull. Without uttering a sound, the soldiers instantly went limp, and Cameron quickly laid him down. He then grabbed him under the armpits and pulled him behind a mound of ice. He waited for him to stop breathing and then immediately started stripping the clothes off the soldiers, all the way down to and including the boots. Once he had his uniform on, Cameron covered the soldier's nude body with ice where it couldn't be seen.

He put the rope he had brought with him over his shoulder and slowly made his way to the top of the structure, taking one floor at a time while looking for Kirstin simultaneously. He made sure none of the other soldiers recognized him as not being one of their own as he kept a low profile. While he circled to the top of the building, he thought, "I hope no one tries to stop me and talk to me, or my cover will be blown." He was lucky because everyone, except the guards on duty, was asleep, and the guards couldn't see his face in the dark. There were several guards stationed throughout the building on each floor.

He finally made it to the top, and after looking around for a few minutes, he finally saw Kirstin's head peeking out of a Russian sleeping bag. She was alive, but her feet and hands were bound with rope, and she had a gag in her mouth so that she couldn't scream. There was another female prisoner who was sitting next to her.

They had a lone guard watching them, and feeling they were securely tied; he looked sleepy and not very responsive. Once he had located Kirstin, he started to look around for a place to tie off the rope and throw it over the edge. Once he had a home located, he casually walked over to the edge of the building as if he were getting some fresh air. He looked around to make sure none of the other guards were watching. He quickly tied the rope securely and threw it over the edge of the building. The entire time, he appeared calm and collected because his training in the Special Forces had kicked in.

Thomas whispered to the team that the rope was thrown over the edge of the building. He said, "Ok, there's the rope, so get ready. It won't be long now." Everyone had their weapons loaded and ready.

Cameron moved closer to Kirstin and the other girl prisoner and got their attention. When Kirstin first saw him, she got wide-eyed, and tears instantly started streaming down her face. Cameron motioned for her and the other prisoner to stay low until he could kill the guard. He put his finger over his lips as if for them to be quiet.

He slowly approached the guard like he was the guard, relieving him of his duty. When he got close enough to the guard, he motioned for him that he would take over as the guard. The soldier started talking to Cameron in Russian, and when Cameron didn't answer him back, the soldier looked a little startled. Before the soldier had time to react, Cameron already had his knife out and leaned forward and plunged it deep underneath the soldier's chin and into his brain. As he started to drop, Cameron put his hand over the soldier's mouth so that he wouldn't make any sounds. Once Cameron knew he was dead, he immediately cut Kirstin and the other girl free and took the gags out of their mouths. He whispered to them not to say anything and to stay low and head for the rope and repeal down it. Once they were down, he told them to go to the other side of the street, where the group awaited them.

A soldier was staffing a 50-caliber machine-gun that was just around the corner from where they were being held captive, and he couldn't see what Cameron had just done to his comrade. Cameron whispered for them to head to the rope because the soldier had his attention on the eastern part of the town and not toward them. Cameron swiftly snuck up behind him and hit him in the back of the head with the butt of his weapon. Cameron quickly grabbed and let him down slowly as he started to drop.

The girls had reached the rope and were on their way down as Cameron immediately turned the 50-caliber machine gun around and fired off about 100 rounds into the additional guards and sleeping soldiers that were lying in their sleeping bags. Cameron was already on the rope and heading down when the soldiers realized what was happening. When he got to the bottom, a few soldiers were leaning over the wall and starting to fire down toward the snowy street in their direction. Thomas and the rest of the group immediately opened fire on soldiers and were able to kill a few of them by the time Cameron and Kirstin had made it across the street to join the group. The soldier's bullets hit the other girl who was lying in the middle of the road, and she wasn't moving. There was nothing Cameron could do for her.

When Kirstin saw Thomas, she ran to him and started hanging onto him as tight as possible. The two teams split up once again as they made their way back to the apartment. They could hear sirens and ATVs searching for them on the way there. Cameron told everyone they needed to move quickly before the soldier spotted them.

It was a crazy plan, but it had worked, at least for now, and they had Kirstin back with them. Now, they just had to figure out how all of them would keep from getting caught in the apartment and killed by the soldiers.

Cameron said, "Man, I feel bad for the poor girl we tried to save. We almost had her home free and with us. That was the craziest thing I've ever done in my life and one time, I thought I was going to die."

Kirstin shook uncontrollably as she approached Cameron, hugged him, and replied, "Thank you, Cameron. I thought I was done for, so thank you again for saving my life."

Cameron chuckled. "We couldn't just let them kill you. We've gotten attached to you."

Everyone laughed nervously as they tried to relax and reflect on their actions. The group took turns watching to ensure no soldiers were hot on their trail as they started getting things ready to leave. Cameron told them they had to leave before the soldiers showed up. He said, "That creek filled about two feet in just the past few days. I don't think the soldiers will be able to cross it soon, but they still can now. Eventually, all the slushy water and ice will break loose at the top of Questa Grade, and once it does, it'll come down on top of this town and destroy everything in its path. The ice and water will eventually run us out if the soldiers don't find us. It's just a matter of time. Maybe we can get lucky and get out of here before they find us and kill us."

Cameron suggested that Thomas and Jason go check out the Pismo Beach area while the rest got things packed and ready to go. He believed the soldiers would be on their way to their apartment once they realized where they'd found Kirstin hiding out. He told Thomas, "We can't waste any time, so try to make it back here as soon as possible because we don't have much time. You must also watch for Soldiers because they'll be everywhere soon."

Thomas and Jason immediately filled the snowmobile tanks and headed south toward Pismo. Once they arrived at Shell Beach, they noticed something strange. The ice had already decreased more than half its original height in those areas along the coastline. After they went along the beach towns, they found that all along with the inland towns, the ice was starting to melt a lot faster than it was inland. Fast-melting ice was the normal process of melting caused by the sun, plus the moist air being blown in from the ocean condensing over the ice pack, which helped release the heat in the ice and speed up the melting process. Vast amounts of water came down from the higher levels and poured into the ocean.

There are many nice hotels along the coastline built upon the cliffs, so Thomas and Jason started to explore them cautiously, one at a time. After going through a few of them, they found where the Russian soldiers had been there and destroyed or damaged the hotel's interior. It also appeared they had abandoned the area and moved further inland for more survivors. Thomas and Jason believed they had moved their forces to San Luis Obispo.

After searching through the large cliff hotels and not finding any soldiers, they believed this would be a perfect place for their group to set up their new hiding place. Some larger hotels are two to four stories high and are excellent places to stay hidden while watching out for soldiers. Once they were convinced this was the place for them, they headed back toward the apartment in San Luis Obispo.

While exploring the beach towns, Cameron, Staci, and Karmen got everything packed and ready to go. They started to get anxious while waiting for Thomas and Jason to return, so they decided to go down toward town to see if the now overflowing banks blocked the soldiers, but they found that it was still passable by the soldiers. Cameron knew the soldiers wouldn't give up looking for them until they found them, but they headed back toward the apartment without seeing any soldiers.

They spotted an entire squad of soldiers searching a few streets over from where their apartment was located on the way back to the apartment. They were frantically searching for them from house to house and apartment to apartment.

Cameron whispered to Staci and Karmen, "Looks like they have a general area where our hideout is, but I am unsure of the exact location. We need to get back to the apartment as quickly as possible, get our stuff loaded up, and get out of there. Stay low, and hopefully, they won't see us."

They got about two hundred yards away from the apartment when one of the soldiers spotted them and opened fire. They heard the bullets fly over their heads as they made the familiar zinging sounds. Cameron yelled for the two girls to cover and set up behind mounds of ice about twenty yards apart. As the soldiers came after them, he told

Staci and Karmen to hold their fire until they were about forty yards away. Once he felt they were close enough, he yelled for the girls to return fire with their M-16 rifles. In their initial volley, they were able to take out some of the advancing soldiers. Now, the three of them were trying to hold off the remaining soldiers of the squad.

When Thomas and Jason got closer to the apartment, they heard the gunfire and believed the Russians had found their hideout and had attacked their group.

Thomas said, "We have to get there and help them out, so let's circle behind the soldiers and catch them in a crossfire. They won't have any hiding place, but watch your back carefully."

Jason went down one street over from the firefight, while Thomas went down another street over. When they were about a hundred yards behind the soldiers, they got off their snowmobiles and stayed low as they each found a mound of ice not too far behind them. The Russians were firing before Thomas and Jason from behind a large ice bank. They could see that Cameron, Staci, and Karmen were able to kill or wound several soldiers before they had gotten there.

Once they were in position, Thomas waived Jason to open fire. They put their weapons on automatic and pulled the triggers. With the first burst of gunfire, a lot of the soldiers went down. The remaining soldiers didn't know what to do as they scurried for another hiding place. They look like mice when you turn on a light, and they don't know which way to go. After several minutes of heavy small-arms fighting, Cameron's group and Thomas and Jason were able to kill or wound what was left of the soldiers' squad. Once the heavy gunfire was over, the guys then went around, killing the remaining wounded soldiers.

Cameron looked around, and when he saw that Karmen had been shot and wasn't moving. As soon as he got a chance to check on her, he saw that she had been shot in the head.

Now, they had lost another one of the precious members of their group. Staci was crying as Cameron picked up Karmen's body while Staci grabbed her weapon, and they headed up the street to the apartment. Thomas and Jason returned, retrieved their snowmobiles, and returned to the apartment.

Thomas told Cameron that he and Jason had found a hotel along the beach for them to stay.

Cameron said, "Man, that was perfect timing, guys. You saved us. We have things packed and ready to go. We'll have to put Karmen's body in the apartment before we leave. The Russians will be sending out re-enforcements soon."

Once back at the apartment, they gathered for a few minutes, said a quick prayer for Karmen, and thanked her for being a good friend and supporting the group. They wrapped her body in a blanket and left her in the garage.

***

Chapter 16

The sun had just come up when the group made it over the hill from San Luis Obispo toward the small town of Pismo Beach, and they could see the beautiful blue water of the Pacific Ocean. It was a welcome sight as Staci said, "Look at that sparkling water; it's breathtaking. I'd forgotten just how beautiful the ocean is." Everyone was happy to see something besides the tops of buildings and trees sticking out thick layers of ice. They were excited to get to the Hotel and check out the one Thomas and Jason had picked out for them.

They had chosen the four-star Dolphin Bay Inn Hotel along Shell Beach Road in Pismo Beach. Before the storm, tourists used it as a five-star luxurious hotel getaway. They believed it would be the perfect place for the group to stay, not just because it was one of the most excellent hotels in the area but because of its ideal location where they could protect themselves. They believed it would be easier to spot enemy soldiers trying to sneak up on them.

When they arrived at the hotel, they hid the snowmobiles behind an ice wall at the hotel's end. They were cautious as they looked around to ensure no soldiers lingered in or near the hotel. They began going through the rooms individually and checking things out. They started on the first floor and worked up to higher levels. As they went through the hotel, they realized that the Russians had thrashed almost every room when they stayed there.

Once they were satisfied that it was safe and free of enemy soldiers, they decided to take two suite rooms connected to the second floor. Each room they picked had a living room, a small kitchenette, two bedrooms, two baths, and two king-size beds in each room.

Staci looked around and laughed, saying, "This may not be home, but it's good enough for me."

Kirstin replied, "Yeah, I love it; this place is amazing."

Cameron and Staci took one room, and Thomas, Kirstin, and Jason took the other room.

Their rooms had a great view of the ocean on the west side and the mountains on the east side. However, it would be hard to see very far in either direction because it sometimes got foggy along the coastline in the early morning hours. Although it gave them a great view in different directions, they must be vigilant if the soldiers tried to sneak up on them. They didn't have running water but had become used to boiling their drinking water and water to pour down the toilets. They could now bathe in the ocean just down the cliff from the hotel.

They took time and cleaned up the two rooms so they looked the way they were before the Russians ransacked the place. They could hunt down clean bedding for the beds, get rid of broken furniture, and replace it with good condition. Once satisfied with how things looked, they returned to relax for a few minutes. However, it wasn't long before they were back, taking turns and watching for enemy soldiers.

On the west side of the hotel, a cliff has a winding walkway path that zig-zagged around and down the few hundred feet drop to the sandy beach below. Once down the ridge, the ocean was just a stone's throw away. The beach stretched for miles south of the hotel, past the Pismo Pier and a few more small towns.

Over the next few days, they came up with signals for each other when someone was down on the beach or when the soldiers were approaching their location so they could notify each other. They also came up with plans on what they would do if the soldiers attacked them inside or outside the hotel.

They would have to hunt for food as needed, but plenty of Coffin Houses were in the foothills, and they could get whatever they wanted and needed from them.

Life was good over the next few weeks as they enjoyed their new home, occasionally taking turns and walking along the beach. They didn't venture far for fear of the enemy seeing and attacking them. They always had someone on the cliff overlooking the ocean as a lookout while walking. For the first time since the storm hit, they could relax a little and not feel threatened by the Russians.

Every few days, the guys would take turns, get on the snowmobiles, and go south to Grover Beach to see if they could find survivors. On one of those trips on the sixth day, Thomas and Jason were near the pier at Pismo Beach when they spotted a couple of young women. They couldn't believe their eyes when they saw the two young women darting from one ice mound to another. They saw Thomas and Jason and began running as if to escape them. The guys wanted to check them out and see if they could talk to women as they headed in their direction.

When the girls saw Thomas and Jason approaching them on the snowmobiles, they stopped near one of the buildings and stood to look at them. As the guys got a little closer, the girls bolted as if they were going to take off running for shelter once again.

Jason ran his snowmobile in front of one of them and yelled, "Hey, hold on, we're not going to hurt you. You don't have to be afraid of us. We aren't Russians. We're survivors of the storm and just looking for other survivors."

When he said that, the girls stopped running and turned around as if they wanted to hear what Jason had to say. One girl spoke up and said, "Ok, if you're not Russian soldiers wanting to kill us, then what do you want with us? "

Jason replied, "We're Americans, just like you, and we're just looking for survivors of the storm to see if we can help them."

The girls appeared to be in their late teens or early twenties, and Jason thought they might be college students. They were both cute girls with dark hair and looked as though they might be alethic because they were thin and fit.

The girl standing in front of Jason said, "Don't you know there are Russian soldiers all around here that want to kill us?"

Jason replied, "Yeah, we know all about the soldiers. We've already had several run-ins with them. We've even killed a lot of them."

Jason gave them a brief rundown of his story of surviving at Walmart. They talked for a few minutes before Jason asked if there was a place where they could talk and exchange stories about how each survived the storm. Thomas and Jason were curious about how these two girls were able to keep from being killed by the soldiers, especially since they hadn't spotted any other survivors in the area since they'd gotten to Pismo.

The girls had the two follow them to a bench table on the Pier that wasn't ice-covered. The Pier extended out over the water about two hundred yards. Thomas and Jason parked the snowmobiles and walked out on the Pier with the girls. They had their weapons strapped over their shoulders with a clip in the chamber as they sat opposite the girls and began to listen to the girl's story.

One girl said, "You guys look well-armed and able to take care of yourselves if you run into the soldiers." Thomas replied, "It's just a matter of survival; we don't like having to use our weapons, but you have to be ready if you get attacked by the Russian soldiers." She continued, "We'd given up trying to find anyone alive until you two showed up today."

We worked at the local winery east of town, off Airport Drive, when the storm hit. We got into one of the wine cellars and set up a place to stay warm enough to survive the freezing temperatures. It was pure hell for those days and nights. I don't know how we made it; it was just pure luck."

Jason replied, "I don't think you could've survived that storm by being lucky. You must have been getting heat from somewhere to stay warm."

She said, "Yes, we had a large generator to keep running, and it saved us."

Thomas didn't say anything but wondered about her story because their group had two of the generators in the mountains, and when it got freezing, both generators froze up and wouldn't run.

"Once we were able to dig our way out and looked around, we started hearing gunfire. We made our way into town and saw what the soldiers were doing to anyone they caught alive. We got scared and went back to the winery and have been hiding out there and just hoping the Russians didn't find and kill us. When the soldiers looked for survivors, we found a place to hide in the cellar, and they didn't find us. We've been afraid to leave there because we didn't want the soldiers to do what they've done to all the other survivors."

Thomas thought, "There's something that doesn't sound right to me with their story. The generators' story was there, and the soldiers were usually comprehensive when looking for survivors. He wondered how they could've missed seeing them in the wine cellar?" Even though he had some reservations and questions about their story, the girl was very convincing.

Jason told them he was impressed they survived the storm when he said, "We're staying at the Dolphin Bay if you girls want to come and stay with us. If you decide to, we'll clean up one of the rooms so you can have your room. We have one other guy and two girls at the hotel with us right now. That's part of our group."

The girl spoke up and said, "Are we safe from the soldiers there with your group?"

Thomas said, "I think so. We are well-armed and can give the soldiers a good fight if we get attacked, so you'll be a lot safer there than where you are now. You don't have any weapons on you, and if we'd been Russian soldiers, we could've killed you. We believe the soldiers have moved further inland in search of more survivors to kill. It appears they've already killed everyone along with these coastal towns. We have automatic rifles, bows, and arrows to protect ourselves against the soldiers. We've already killed a huge number of them when they attacked us over the past few months."

Just for an instant, there was a frown on the face of one of the girls. Thomas saw her frown and said, "Yeah, it may seem gross to have to kill another person, but sometimes you don't have much choice. They're trying to kill us, so we have to defend ourselves." The girl didn't say anything; she seemed repulsed by what they heard.

The other girl said, "Let us talk to each other about going with you guys, and we'll let you know in a few minutes."

The girls talked alone with each other and, in a few minutes, said they believed it might be better if they went with them instead of going it alone.

The girl said, "If it's ok with you, we need to go back to the winery to get a few of our things to take with us."

The guys agreed, and Jason replied, "Once you're part of our group, you girls will have to help us hunt for food and help out with other chores."

They both chimed in about the same time and said, "No problem, we can do that."

They had the girls jump on the back of the snowmobile and head to the winery to get their items. The guys waited outside as they gave the girls time to get what they needed.

When the girls were inside, Thomas said to Jason; there's something fishy about their story. I can't quite put my finger on it, but my gut tells me something about their story doesn't sound right. We may want to be a bit extra vigilant with them.

Jason said, "Come on, I think you're getting paranoid."

Once the girls had everything, they loaded it on the snowmobiles and returned to Dolphin Bay.

When they arrived at the hotel, the girls were excited, and one of them said, "This is impressive; it must be one of the nicest hotels in this area. We've been by this place before but never stayed here."

Jason puffed out his chest and said, "Yeah, Thomas and I picked it out, and it's pretty nice, so come on in, and we'll introduce you to the rest of the group. After you meet everyone, we'll get you a room."

The rest of the group had seen them arrive, and they were waiting in the room and standing guard. Cameron was a little standoffish when Thomas and Jason came in with the two girls as they introduced themselves as Malory and Jessica. They told everyone they were Softball players at Cal Poly before the storm hit.

Malory said, "When it hit, we worked at the local Wine Tasting Winery just south of town.

Malory was five feet seven inches tall with dark brown hair and green eyes. Jessica was about the same height and had dark brown hair and brown eyes. They spent about an hour and told everyone exactly how they survived the storm and how they evaded the Russian Soldiers when they came looking for survivors.

Staci tried to talk about their families, but the girls avoided any questions regarding them. Staci thought it might be because they didn't want to face the fact that their parents were now dead from the storm or were in denial. Staci thought it seemed strange because she didn't know the girls were concerned about losing their family members in the storm. She didn't say anything to anyone about how she was feeling and kept her feelings to herself.

After listening to them and talking it over with everyone, Cameron welcomed the girls to the group, saying, "We're glad to have you girls as part of our group. It should be like a vacation for you girls compared to the hell you've already gone through at the winery. You deserve a little rest from the hiding place where you've been staying. We'll help protect you."

Things were going smoothly for the group for the next few weeks, and everyone enjoyed not worrying about being killed. They hadn't seen any soldiers and felt comfortable with their new home. Everyone was hanging out together and getting to know Malory and Jessica. The three of them had been going to the beach as much as they could and hanging out by the water. Living there was like being on vacation except for some inconveniences and the soldiers' constant threat.

When Jason wasn't with them, Jessica and Malory spent much of their time alone when they weren't down at the beach. They kept to themselves and in their room most of the time. Once in their room, they didn't socialize much with the rest of the group. Sometimes, Staci and Kirstin would talk about it and couldn't figure out why the girls didn't want to spend more time with everyone else. They were starting to wonder if the two girls were a couple, so Staci asked Malory about it.

She laughed and said, "No way, we're just good friends, and we've been friends for a long time. The storm made us bond more because we had to rely on each other to stay alive. I'm sorry if we seem disconnected from the rest of the group, but we just got used to spending time together."

Just like a lot of other things in life, when it seems like things can't get any better in your life, then that's when things start to unravel and fall apart. It was a nice, bright, sunny day, and Jason decided to go down to the beach with Jessica and Malory because they would spend the day with each other. They had a favorite huge rock they liked to hang out on and soak up the sun. It was about thirty feet in diameter and twelve feet high, perfect for sunbathing.

After sitting on the rock and talking for a few hours, Jason pranks the girls. He got up and told them he was returning to the hotel for a while, but I'd return in about an hour. The girls said okay and that they would see him later. Jason climbed down from the top of the rock and headed toward the trail. The girls watched until they thought he'd returned up the cliff to be with the rest of the group. He pretended to go back as he circled down and crept up behind the rock below where the girls were sitting. He had a plan that, at the right moment, he would jump out and scare them.

He had a crush on Malory, so he would wait and hear what they had to say before he jumped out at them. He hoped she might say she liked him or something good about him, and maybe they could build a relationship. He crouched behind the huge rock below them and listened intently to their conversation.

As he sat there listening, he was frozen in place as he heard the girls speaking to each other in Russian. At first, he couldn't believe his ears and tried to wrap his head around what he was hearing. After listening for several minutes, he heard the girls start talking in English. They said something about how they had to meet back up with their soldiers in San Luis Obispo soon. He heard them say that they would have to kill everyone in Cameron's group before meeting their comrades. Jason turned around and put his back on the rock as he raised his head and rolled his eyes. He couldn't believe what he'd just heard.

Once he heard their plan, Jason knew he had to stay hidden to ensure they didn't see him. He knew they would've found a way to kill him and make it look like an accident if they knew he heard what they had planned. He thought, "These damn girls are just Russian agents that were planted here to kill all of us." He felt a little stupid that he had fallen for all their lies.

In a little while, the girls went back to the hotel, so Jason waited about ten minutes and then made his way up the cliffs to the hotel. Once he knew the girls were in their room alone, he tapped on the door of Cameron and Staci's room. Staci was standing guard duty as Cameron came to the door. Not knowing if the girls had bugged their rooms, Jason put his finger over his mouth to tell Cameron to be quiet. Jason told Cameron to come with him because he had something to say. Cameron wondered what kind of prank Jason was trying to pull but went along. He then opened the door to where Thomas was and motioned for him to follow them. When he saw Thomas, he put his finger over his mouth to tell him to be quiet.

Thomas had seen that look on Jason's face before and automatically knew something was wrong. Jason didn't say anything, so Thomas and Cameron quickly followed Jason to an empty room down the hallway. Before they were inside, Jason looked down the hallway to ensure the girls hadn't seen them enter that room. Once inside, he quietly closed the door behind them.

Thomas looked at Jason and whispered, "Hey, man, what's happening with you? You look like you've just seen a ghost. Did you spot some soldiers, or what?"

Jason softly said, "You won't believe this, but those two girls are not Americans. They're Russian soldiers. When I was down at the beach earlier, I played a trick on them, so I hid behind a rock and heard them speaking to each other in Russian. I also overheard them talking in English about killing all of us and meeting up with their comrades in San Luis Obispo once they carried out their mission."

Cameron immediately got angry as he replied, "Those damn Russians, I knew it, I knew there was something strange about those girls. They sure are tricky, and they will do anything to try and kill their enemy. This entire time, the Russians had put them here as plants to lure us into a trap to kill us. Their plan worked perfectly because we accepted them with open arms."

Jason had been spending a lot of time with the girls and knew them better than the rest of the group, so they had no reason to question if what Jason was telling them was true or not.

Cameron said, "Man, it's a good thing you found out about their plan before they cut all our throats or blew our brains out when we least expected it. I wonder what they have planned to try and kill us?"

Jason said, "I don't know. I didn't hear them say their plan, just that they would do it soon."

Cameron replied, "We have to do something tonight before they can put their plan into effect. It doesn't matter how we kill the girls; the Russians will send out soldiers to find out what happened to them, especially if they don't hear from them in a few days. I wonder how they've communicated with their commanding officer since they've been here. They must have some way they're communicating. We'll have to be prepared to fight the soldiers in a few days when they come looking for their girls. Once we kill the girls, we'll set up a trap for the soldiers they send after us. Jason, tell the girls they must go with you to get food tonight. Once you're ready, I'll meet you out front and tell the three of you that I'm going with you. We'll take care of them once we get food at one of the Coffin Houses. Once we kill them, we'll start getting things ready and move over to the Cliffs Resort next door. I'm sure the girls have already told their commanding officers about us and everything about our hideout here at the Dolphin Bay. The girls have probably given them where the entrances, rooms, exits, and everything else are located. The rooms and everything at the Cliffs are as nice as the Dolphin Bay. From those rooms, we'll still be able to watch for the soldiers they send after us. When they get here, they'll be thinking we're still at the Dolphin Bay, and they'll run into our trap."

Cameron didn't want to tell Staci or Kirstin about their plan to kill the two girls for fear they would become too emotional about it and try to talk them out of killing them. He told Jason and Thomas what they'd say to them once the girls were dead.

After their meeting, Jason went directly to Malory and Jessica's room and told them they needed to go with him later that night to get food. They had been out with him before, so it wasn't a big surprise to them that he wanted them to go with him. He told them to be ready when it got dark. They cheerfully replied they'd be prepared. Jason was thinking, "Man, they probably have plans to kill me tonight. They were too ready and willing to go with me to get food."

For the rest of the day, Jason stayed in his room, and he was angry that they had deceived him and the rest of the group. He trusted them and honestly believed they were just who they said they were and needed protection. Now, his mind was going wild. The more he thought about it, the happier he was that Cameron was going with him. He shivered at the thought of one of them cutting his throat. Jason was starting to think he should go down to their room and kill them before they had a chance to carry out their plans for him. Then he realized he didn't want Kirstin and Staci to see their bodies after he killed them. He decided to stick to the plan he and Cameron had initially agreed to because he knew the two of them would have to be watching each other backs.

Cameron and Jason ensured they had their weapons loaded and ready to fire just before Jason met up with the girls. Once outside, he stalked around outside for a few minutes before they were prepared to leave the hotel.

Cameron exited his room and said, "Hey guys, wait up. I want to go with you if that's ok."

Jason said, "If you want to, that would be great. You can show us where we need to go."

The girls looked at each other and shrugged as if they were okay with that.

The entire time they were looking for a Coffin House to go into, Cameron and Jason kept the two girls between them so they could keep an eye on them. They were gone for about an hour when they found a house that Cameron thought might suit their plan. He whispered to Jason to keep his weapon ready as he had Jason and the girls dig down through the ice to the door. Jason busted the door open and had his flashlight in his hand as he looked around the house. Jason told the girls it looked safe, so they could go into the kitchen area and start putting cans of food and other things in the backpacks they brought with them.

The girls were busy putting food in the backpack when Jason and Cameron calmly walked behind them. They had their pistols in their hands as Cameron said several words in Russian that he'd learned from Rachel. The girls immediately stopped what they were doing and stiffened up. They still had their backs to Cameron and Jason as each of them reached for a weapon they had strapped to their bodies inside their clothes.

Two shots instantly rang out as Jason and Cameron did just as they had planned and shot the girls in the back of the head. They immediately fell to the floor and jerked around briefly as they took their last breaths. Cameron saw that Jessica already had a pistol in her hand, and Malory was reaching for her gun when Jason shot her.

Cameron looked down at the two of them and said, "We got lucky, Jason. These girls had their plan to kill us tonight."

Jason took a deep breath and said, "Man, that's scary. I could be dead right now if I hadn't heard about their plan to kill us. The Russians must be wanting us pretty bad to send out plants like them to infiltrate our group."

When Cameron and Jason returned to the hotel about an hour later, they told Staci and Kirstin the girls were Russian agents and what they had planned. He said, "They had pistols strapped inside their clothing and to their bodies and were getting ready to use them against us before we killed them."

Staci said, "So what happened to them?"

Cameron replied, "Jason and I killed them before they got a chance to kill us. We left their bodies in the house where we shot them.

"Staci was shaken as she said, "I knew their story about how they survived didn't add up to me because they never would talk about their loved ones. I should've said something to you then about my concerns, but I didn't. They just seemed so sincere."

Thomas said, "Hey, Staci, when we first met them, their story seemed off to me, but I didn't say anything either."

Cameron replied, "Don't worry about it. They fooled all of us because they were good at what they did, but from now on, we'll talk to each other when we have a gut feeling about someone. We just got lucky this time that Jason heard them talking about their plan to kill all of us."

Cameron said, "I know those girls had some way they were communicating with their commanders. Tomorrow morning, let's go through everything in their room until we find what it is and where it is. Cameron was angry with himself when they went to bed that night because he'd let the girls deceive him. He didn't like the idea of killing them but knew they had no choice because it was a case of killing or being killed.

The group carefully went through everything in the girls' room when they got up the following day. They pulled out every piece of clothing and everything else the girls possessed. They lifted the beds and looked under the mattresses. They tipped over the furniture to see if anything had been hidden. They went into the bathroom and went through all their items, and there was still nothing to be found. Finally, Cameron unscrewed the vent plate in the living room, and there it was. It was like a walkie-talkie radio; they had taken the batteries out of it and laid them aside so they didn't receive any incoming calls when they didn't want them.

Cameron knew why the Russians had picked those two girls; they spoke perfect English and were trained well. They were both compelling. Cameron's group now had the communication device, but it was of little value because none understood Russian. Cameron knew some words but not enough to understand a complete conversation with their command center.

Cameron said, "Ok, now we know they had contact with their commander, so we must prepare for a confrontation with the soldiers again. We need to head to the camp in San Luis Obispo tomorrow and get another box of grenades. We'll also get some more bandoleers of M-16 ammunition. You girls get ready to move our things over to the Cliff Resort and grab a couple of adjoining rooms with a view so we can see the soldiers when they come looking for their girls and us."

Once they checked everything on the snowmobiles, the guys headed north toward San Luis Obispo. It was about 10 miles there and then another 13 miles north/west to the base and the warehouse. It would take at least an hour and a half each way.

When they arrived at the warehouse, they knew where things were located, so it didn't take long to get the box of grenades and additional ammunition and get out of there quickly. They were on their way back and had made it just south of San Luis Obispo near the Madonna Inn Hotel when something happened to Jason's snowmobile. It stopped running and completely shut down. They pulled over and tried to get it working again, but after 15 minutes of not getting anywhere, they decided to leave it there. Jason jumped on the back of Thomas's snowmobile and put the grenades' box and extra ammunition on Cameron's snowmobile.

By the time they returned to Dolphin Bay, Staci and Kirstin had moved everything to the Cliff Resort Hotel. They picked a couple of adjoining rooms on the third floor that had a great view of the entrance and parking area of both the Cliff Resort Hotel and the Dolphin Bay parking lot. They could keep a good watch for the Russians from there. The rooms weren't the suites like the Dolphin Bay, but they were still nice and comfortable, and each had big king-size beds.

Cameron told everyone about his plans to ambush the Russians once they arrived. He said, "I think we should booby trap everything we can in and around the Dolphin Bay hotel. Maybe we can kill several of them before we engage them with our small arms weapons. We'll keep some of the grenades to throw at them once we get into the firefight with them.

Over the next few days, the guys dug foxholes in the ice and had little mounds of ice in front of the foxholes where they could brace their weapons and shoot from there. They had a foxhole for each of them.

It was just starting to get dark on the evening of the eighth day after the girls were killed during Staci's guard duty. She noticed activity from about two hundred yards away. Soldiers were creeping along and staying low along the ice as they headed toward Dolphin Bay.

Staci immediately yelled to everyone, "Hey guys, they're here! The soldiers are here!"

Everyone immediately jumped up and ran to the window to get a look and see for themselves. About twelve of them were making their way in their direction.

Cameron said, "Ok, everyone, you know what we're going to do, so get your weapons and ammunition, and let's head down to our position. Before they left the room, he told Thomas and Jason not to forget their grenades. Everyone was apprehensive but knew what to do as they left the Cliff Resort Hotel and low-crawled over to their designated foxhole.

They waited for what seemed like forever once they reached their foxhole. Finally, Cameron's group heard an explosion from one of the booby-trap grenades inside Dolphin Bay. They continued to listen to a few more explosions, and then there was silence. The soldiers lost four of the original twelve men before they realized they had been ambushed. When they came out of the hotel, they raised their weapons and aimed right and left in front of them as they looked around to see if they could see anyone.

They seemed to be trying to regroup as Cameron yelled at the group's command to fire on them. Instantly, two of the soldiers went down from the heavy gunfire from Cameron's group. The remaining soldiers had taken cover and were firing back at the group. The firefight went on for several minutes when Cameron pulled the pin to a couple of his grenades and tossed them toward the soldier's position. The first explosion stopped a couple of the soldiers from firing back as they were hit with the grenade blast. Then Thomas and Jason each threw a couple of their grenades in the direction of the soldiers. Every time the soldiers started firing at them, Cameron's group would throw grenades in that direction. The fighting continued for several more minutes until all the firing from the other side eventually stopped altogether.

Cameron and Thomas slowly got out of their foxholes and watched for a few minutes to see if there was movement from any soldiers. A few were squirming around and screaming out in pain as the guys approached them and put a bullet in their heads.

Everyone now knew they were in deep trouble because they'd killed all twelve of the soldiers that were sent there to kill them. Cameron said, "Looks like we have to decide pretty soon. Do we wait here for them to send more troops to come after us, or do we go elsewhere?"

They kept a guard on duty all night just if the Russians sent out more soldiers during the night.

The next day, they went through the Dolphin Bay hotel, retrieved the grenades that hadn't exploded, and put them away if needed. The guys loaded up the dead soldier bodies, one by one, and took them to "Coffin Houses" and left their bodies inside.

***

Chapter 17

Three days after the guys disposed of the soldier's bodies, it was a cold morning. The fog had rolled in like it often does that time of year, along with the coastal towns. Jason was on guard duty and heard a lot of activity from a short distance from the hotel. The noise was coming from somewhere past what he could see because of the dense fog. He immediately woke everyone and informed them he believed someone was approaching their position. He told everyone to grab their weapons because it sounded like the Russians were coming after them with a large group of soldiers.

As the noise got louder, they soon could tell an entire company of soldiers was marching into the hotel's parking lot. As Cameron's group watched the soldiers, they could mean something different about this group of men. They weren't hiding from anything or anyone, and they looked confident in what they were doing.

After a few minutes, Cameron said, "Hey, I think those guys are American soldiers. They have American flags and look and act like Americans on their ATVs."

Staci replied, "Do you think they are, or do you think they may be just wearing American Uniforms to try and draw us out into the open? Those Russians are smart and crafty, and we already found that out when they tricked us with the two girls."

Cameron replied, "Let's watch them for a few minutes and see what they're doing here."

The soldiers started setting up a few tents and awnings in the Parking lot, and a Captain was giving orders.

Cameron looked at everyone and asked, "Are you ready to confront the group? I'm going to yell down to them and see what happens." Everyone gripped their rifles with much anticipation of a fight.

Cameron opened the window that looked out over the parking area and yelled. "Hey, Yankees, what are you doing in our parking lot?" He said that the entire company of soldiers took cover with their rifles aimed up in Cameron's direction. Not getting an answer, Cameron shouted out again, "Hey, we're Americans, don't shoot us." He figured if they were Russians, they would open fire on him when he said that.

The Captain spoke up and asked Cameron what they were doing there. He was a young officer about six-foot-tall with the typical Army short-cut hair and short along with the ears. He was dressed in a clean army green uniform.

Cameron yelled back to him, "We survived the huge storm and have been fighting Russian soldiers every place we've been."

The Captain said, "What the hell are you guys doing here?"

Cameron told him they were hiding from the Russian soldiers and trying to stay alive.

Cameron was reluctant to tell him only five were in their group. He said, "We're well-armed and ready to fight if necessary."

The Captain said, "We didn't think there were any survivors left around here because we haven't seen any in the area."

Cameron replied, "Yeah, I think the Russians have killed all of them they come across. We've been here about four weeks now, and the only people we've seen have been Russians that we killed. How do we know you're not a Russian soldier disguised as an American soldier sent here to try and kill us, too?"

The Captain said, "I'm Captain Roger Singletary, and these soldiers are all part of my company. We're Company A of the 2nd battalion of the 101 Airborne Division of the United States Army. We've been dispatched from Area 51 to find the Russian soldiers and get them out of our country."

Cameron replied, "Do you know General Thompson from Area 51?"

Captain Singletary said, "Hell yes, he's the one that sent us out here to go after the Russians. How do you know him?"

Cameron said, "He asked our group to help him find the Russians, and he gave us a couple of men and radios so that we could stay in communication with his headquarters. Our radio recently went on the blink, so we haven't been able to contact them."

Captain Singletary said, "I know who you guys are. You're the group from Fresno that's been fighting and killing a lot of the Russians. The last transmission from you to General Thompson said you were heading to San Luis Obispo. He hadn't heard from you in a while, so he told us to find your group and see if you were still alive. I'd love to hear the stories of your fights with those sorry Russians."

Cameron told the Captain they would come down and meet him and his men. The group had their weapons ready to use when they met them, just as if something had gone wrong.

When Cameron was close enough to talk to the Captain without shouting, he said, "We thought you might be Russian soldiers trying to trick us.

The Captain laughed, shook Cameron's hand, and said, "Man, I like how you roll. Don't trust anyone. That's a good way to stay alive. Tell your friends to relax; I'm from Graysville, West Virginia. I'm just about as much of an American as you can get."

Cameron told him that he was from Fresno, California, and the rest of the group was from different California areas.

Cameron signaled everyone that things were right, so they lowered their weapons and slowly approached Cameron, the Captain, and his soldiers.

Once they were together, the Captain said, "You guys are amazing. We haven't found any survivors around here, and yet your group has been killing the Russian soldiers all over this damn state, and you're still alive. I would love for us all to talk and learn about your stories and how you've stayed alive this long and ended up here. Maybe after the men are settled in, the First Sergeant and I can join you in your room and discuss everything.

Cameron told the Captain there were some nice empty rooms at the Cliff Hotel and over at the Dolphin Bay Inn Hotel if they wanted to stay there. He told him their group had been staying at Dolphin Bay until about a week ago when the Russians sent a group of twelve soldiers from San Luis Obispo to kill them.

The Captain asked what happened to them.

Jason then chimed in and calmly said, "We killed all of them, then we disposed of their bodies in some of the Coffin Houses."

The Captain replied, "I'm impressed, but what's a Coffin House?"

Jason replied, "We killed a lot more of them in San Luis Obispo before we moved over here. Coffin Houses are what we call houses where people died in their houses from the storm."

When he said that, Thomas looked over at Cameron and had a slight smile on his face. He didn't like Jason bragging about killing soldiers but didn't say anything to him about it.

The captain said, "I'm Looking forward to hearing all about what you guys have been through."

That night, after Captain Singletary got all his soldiers situated, the group got together with the Captain and his First Sergeant and discussed things. The Captain wanted to hear their stories. Cameron's group was interested in what was going on with the Military. The Captain told them he'd talked to General Thompson's headquarters earlier and told them they had found Cameron's group and were still alive. "General Thompson sent his best regards for your group and said, God bless you, and thank you for helping to get rid of some enemy soldiers."

He told the group the President of the United States had started mobilizing troops all over America. He had deployed fifteen thousand troops along the West Coast, fifteen thousand moving in from Alaska, fifteen thousand from the Southern shores of the United, and fifteen thousand from the East Coast. He said they also had about 50,000 troops from the underground Bases in the United States deployed, and all of them were moving in on the Russian positions.

He told them it was the military's goal to stop the Russians from slaughtering any more of the remaining survivors and take back the country. He said everyone was in place, and it wouldn't be long before they stopped all the killing that was going on by the Russians. He said there were several divisions of American troops all along the West Coast, and they were searching for the Russian headquarters. They aren't looking to take any prisoners, especially after what they've been doing to our people. Thomas and Jason high-fived each other after he told them that. They were happy the government was controlling things and eliminating the killers.

Staci hugged Cameron around the neck and said, "Thank God!"

After discussing everything they'd been through and their encounters with the soldiers, the Captain asked Cameron what his group planned to do next. He asked them if they wanted to continue staying or going with them and showed them where the Russian Headquarters was. He told them he could use their help to find some of their prominent locations since they were familiar with where they were headquartered. He told them they had to be prepared to have more firefights with the soldiers if they went with them. Cameron thought about it and told the Captain they would meet with the five of them and let him know in the morning what their decision would be.

After the Captain and First sergeant left, everyone felt more secure because American troops were retaking control of the country. Cameron told everyone they might be safe if they stayed and did nothing. He said, "Maybe we can help these guys kill the Russians, and we won't have to worry about them coming after us. Who knows for sure? Maybe the Russians will kill the Captain and his men and then come back here and try to kill us? We don't know the answer to those questions, but I would like to be out there with the soldiers, so I know what's going on and not having to look over my shoulder all the time wondering when they were going to sneak up on us and kill us. Knowing the Captain and his men are trying to kill the Russians gives me a lot of hope we can get rid of the Russians."

He knew Thomas and Kirstin were getting along well, but Kirstin wasn't much of a fighter. He told them that if they wanted to stay in the safety and comfort of the hotel, then he understood. He told them he was okay with staying there if they wanted to do that. He told them he believed they would be safe now that the American troops were there.

That night, after they went to bed, Staci and Cameron talked, and Cameron told Staci he felt obligated to go with the American Soldiers and help them. He told Staci she could stay with Thomas and Kirstin if she wanted. That way, she wouldn't have to worry about the soldiers trying to kill her. Staci told him she stayed by his side no matter his decision and hugged him. He hugged her back and thanked her for standing behind him.

The following day, they met and told Thomas, Kirstin, and Jason they were going with the soldiers. Thomas told Cameron he was his best friend, but he didn't want to take any more chances with Kirstin because she wasn't a fighter, and he cared about her and believed he had to try to protect her. He told them that Jason and the two would stay at the hotel. Cameron told Thomas he understood exactly how they felt and didn't blame them or feel bad for their decision to stay.

Cameron then went out to where the Captain was preparing to leave and told him that he and Staci wanted to go with him and his company, and they would show them where the enemy headquarters were located. The captain was happy they would join them and told Cameron and Staci they were leaving in a few hours, so they had to be ready when it was time to leave. They told the Captain they were already packed and ready to go.

They said their goodbyes to Thomas, Kirstin, Jason, and Cameron, pulled Thomas aside and told him he loved him. He thanked them for their help in keeping each other alive over the past few months. He told

Thomas to open a room for them when they returned. They hugged, and Staci and Kirstin shed a few tears before meeting the Captain.

Before they left, Cameron told the Captain they shouldn't go north on the way to San Luis Obispo. He told him the Russians had many soldiers in the downtown area and a central headquarters in the government building downtown. He told him they also have a group of soldiers in and on top of the four-story parking structure just a couple of blocks away from their headquarters. He said the soldiers had been executing the survivors from the top of the parking structure building. He told the Captain how they had killed many of the Soldiers on the building while they were hiding out at Jason's apartment.

He told the Captain that he believed if they planned it outright, they could kill many Russians in those two locations. The Captain asked Cameron how many soldiers he thought were in those two locations. Cameron told him he believed there was an entire battalion of soldiers, less the ones they had already killed. He believed there were about six or seven hundred left. The Captain thought that was a lot since his company only had 124 soldiers. He knew they would have to take their time and figure out the best way to take out their targets.

Before they left, Cameron gave the Captain a detailed drawing of the County building where the Russians had set up their command center. He also gave them the location of the parking structure. Cameron thought that if they tried to come in from the west side of town, they couldn't get across the creek that ran through the city's center. It would now be like a huge river overflowing instead of a little slow-moving creek. He told the Captain he thought his soldiers should go east of Pismo Beach and hook up with Airport Drive that led north/west into town. They could come into San Luis Obispo from the east and avoid some of the problems of trying to approach from the west.

When they got ready to move the company out, the Captain did as Cameron had suggested and headed east. It was only about ten miles, but it took almost a half-day to find Airport Drive. Once there, they regrouped and headed toward San Luis Obispo. It took several more hours to make it to the edge of town with all the men and equipment they carried. It was now after dark, and they needed to find a place to set up camp. They found a large open area across from the Airport, and the Captain had his soldiers set up a perimeter with guards on duty.

Once they were set up and secured, the Captain called up three forward observers as a recon squad to try and observe the enemy. He also wanted them to get the exact map grids on the two target buildings they intended to hit. They were gone for several hours, and it was in the early morning hours when they finally returned with the information the Captain wanted.

The Captain had earlier talked to Cameron, and he gave the Captain information about the surrounding area near the two buildings. The Captain had plans to move his soldiers into a position near the two buildings. He surprised Cameron when he told him he'd been in touch with General Thompson, and they were calling in airstrikes to hit the two buildings before his men would go in and engage any surviving soldiers. Cameron was impressed as he said, "Now we're talking. We'll get those scumbags that have been killing so many innocent people."

Early the following day, Cameron and Staci met with the Captain again as he and the First Sergeant were getting ready to brief his soldiers. The First Sergeant told them they would split into four platoons and move to their target position at night. Two platoons would set up a safe distance from the County building, and two platoons would set up a safe distance from the parking garage structure. He told the soldiers they would leave in the middle of the afternoon and get in position. He told everyone he was calling in airstrikes on the two buildings, and they would arrive from a base in Hawaii at 0600 hours. He told them once they blew up the two structures, the bombing was over. The platoons would then move in on the remaining Russian soldiers and kill them.

Once everything was set and ready to go, he communicated with the United States Air Force commanders from Hickman Air Force Base in Hawaii and gave them the exact location of the two buildings. He instructed them to hit them full force at 0600 hours the following morning.

The two F-22 Fighter bombers from the 27th fighter squadron were loaded with one 2,000-pound bomb and 20 250-pound bombs and headed for San Luis Obispo as Captain Singletary moved his troops into place and waited for the American air attack.

In the early morning, the two planes were right on time as they came in low from a westerly direction. At first, all you could hear off in the distance was a buzzing sound, and then it kept getting louder as it approached its target. One plane hit the County building almost dead center with the 2,000-pound bomb, and the other F-22 crashed the parking structure dead center with its 2,000-pound bomb. The aircraft then circled and hit their targets repeatedly with 250-pound bombs until all the bombs dropped. The massive airstrikes and secondary explosions from Russian ammunition killed most of the Russian Soldiers. There were still a few stragglers who somehow survived the bombing and tried to find a place to hide.

Cameron and Staci were with the Captain when he commanded his soldiers to attack the surviving soldiers. At first, there was a lot of sporadic gunfire between the Russian and American soldiers as the Americans moved in on the two locations. The American soldiers fired several grenade launcher rounds into what was left of the two buildings. There was a lot of small arms fire coming from the Russians that were trying to flee. The fighting lasted for a few hours but gradually dwindled to where there were just occasional bursts of gunfire. After about an hour, the Captain got a message that the mission was over. He got word that they had killed all the soldiers left in the area.

When it was over, the First Sergeant reported to Captain Singletary that they had lost seven soldiers killed and eight wounded in the aftermath of the fighting. The Captain wasn't happy about losing his soldiers but was delighted the mission was successful. He reported to the Air Force Commanders that the bombings had worked, and several hundred of the Russian soldiers had been killed. The Captain had his soldiers gather up the dead American Soldiers and take care of the wounded.

The victory would be short-lived as the Captain got the word that the thunderous noise from bombings had resonated up the canyon to Questa Grade and caused the ice and slush to break free from the mountain, and it was headed down the canyon toward town. It would only be a few hours before the massive wall of ice and slush would flow down into the central part of the city. When he got that information, he started having his men return to the staging area they had set up the day before.

Cameron and Staci had become more like observers during this mission but were happy. They didn't have to worry about being killed.

***

Chapter 18

After regrouping for a few days, Captain Singletary talked to Cameron and Staci and asked them where they thought his company should go next, searching for the enemy. Cameron didn't have to think about it; he told the Captain they believed Fresno would be a good target because the soldiers had another headquarters command post set up in the middle of the old town.

He told the Captain what the Russians had done in Fresno to one of his best friends by skinning him alive and had him hanging upside down from streetlights in the middle of town when they found him. He also told him about his act of revenge against the soldiers when he was angry about what they had done to Brian. He said he'd gone out alone and killed many soldiers during his furious revenge spree. He believed an entire battalion of 700 to 800 enemy soldiers was there.

Staci looked up at Cameron in surprise when he told the Captain about going out alone and killing the soldiers. He had kept that from her, and she wasn't happy. She angrily said, "Why didn't you tell any of us about that? You could've been killed."

Cameron apologized to her and told her he was sorry for not telling her, but it was something he just needed to do alone. She said nothing else and shook her head because she didn't want the Captain to enter their spat.

He told the Captain he wasn't sure if the soldiers were still there because the valley had been filling with water, and there may be several feet below the melting slushy ice by now. He believed there was a possibility the Russians may have already moved into the Sierra mountains or into the Coastal mountain region west of Fresno to get away from the flooding waters. He said they would have to keep an eye open for them just if they had started to retreat into the foothills in the direction they were heading. The Captain told Cameron that from all the reports he was getting from other company forward observers,

Fresno and the valley had become too dangerous to venture into that area. The reports said the Russians headquartered in Fresno had already moved to the small town of Kettleman City. They believed it was a perfect place for the Russians to temporarily set up their new headquarters and pick off survivors as they retreated to higher ground. The Captain's troops would take about a week to arrive based on location.

Staci and Cameron talked about the sole mission he went out on in Fresno and worked it out where everything was good between them. Once they had everything packed, they headed in that direction. Every day, the Captain sent out three soldiers ahead of the rest of the group as forwarding observers to see if they could spot enemy soldiers. They weren't supposed to engage the enemy unless they were ambushed and had no choice. Their main job was reporting any suspicious enemy activity to the Captain.

It was late in the morning of the 6th day of moving further inland when the forward observers came back with the news they'd spotted what looked like an entire battalion of Russian Soldiers camped out in a few of the hotels along the intersection of what used to be Interstate five and Highway 41. They said the Russians had equipment, tents, and awnings in two hotels' parking areas.

When the Captain got that news, he called a meeting with his soldiers to plan their strategy. Cameron told the Captain he'd been using a successful tactic with his small group, which he used in Afghanistan. He told him they had luck in spreading the small group about twenty yards apart and in a half-circle surrounding the enemy position. It made the enemy think they were fighting a larger group of people than what they had. The Captain liked the idea, so he briefed his soldiers on how they would be setting up a perimeter just like Cameron suggested in a half-circle around each side of the hotels. Just before dark, and once they had everything set, they moved out to meet up with their intended target. On the way to their destination, they received sporadic gunfire from the enemy insurgents who must've been out on patrol looking for survivors.

It was dark when they moved four platoons in and set up their fighting position about thirty yards apart and two hundred yards from each hotel. They quickly dug foxholes in the ice to protect them against an enemy attack.

Once the Captain had his soldiers in position, he called in airstrikes for 0600 hours the following day, just as he'd done in San Luis Obispo, except the planes were coming in Elmendorf Air Force Base in Alaska.

They were sending out two F-22s from the 90th fighter squadron loaded with a 2,000-pound bomb and 20 – 250-pound bombs on each plane, just like the ones that had blown up the two buildings in San Luis Obispo.

The Russians knew the American soldiers had moved in and were occasionally firing rockets and mortars in their direction. They also used flares and small arms fire to draw the American soldiers into a fight. The Captain had his soldiers hold their fire until after the airstrikes. He knew they were over-matched in staffing and didn't want to let the Russians know just how many soldiers he had, or maybe they would've tried to overrun his position. He also knew that once the planes dropped their bombs, it would kill a high percentage of them, and then his soldiers could kill the rest.

It was a long night of cat-and-mouse tactics between the Russians and the Americans, but just at daybreak, there was a humming sound in the distance as the two planes headed for their targets. It started with a low growling sound until it became a thunderous roar as they spotted their targets and broke the quiet before the storm as they dropped the 2,000-pound bombs on each of the hotels. They then circled and came back and hit the hotels and parking lots with 250-pound bombs several times until all the bombs had been dropped.

The sound from the bombs was deafening, and some of the Russian ammunition was also exploding. Rockets, mortars, RPGs, and bullets were firing out in a thousand different directions as the American soldiers ducked down into their foxholes for protection. The explosions lasted for several minutes before they started to die down.

The hotels and parking lots were in shambles, but enemy soldiers were still trying to find a place to hide. They were moving from one position to another as they took a few minutes and fired in the American soldiers' direction. Some of them began to head in the direction of the American perimeter, and they were met with heavy small-arms fire and RPGs as the American Soldiers picked them off one by one.

Cameron and Staci were fully armed and had moved into a forward position. They were fighting alongside the American soldiers as they killed the Russian Soldiers as they headed out of the building's rubble. They were doing their part in trying to kill the soldiers who attempted to escape.

Once the fighting ended, the Captain had his soldiers move into the crumbled buildings, searching for surviving Russian soldiers. Cameron and Staci moved in with them as the battle continued for several hours. At times, they were very close to hand-to-hand combat with a few Russian soldiers. It was during the fighting when Staci was hit and knocked off her feet. When the bullet first struck her, it burned as it went completely through her left shoulder. For an instant, she didn't know what had happened as she lay on the ground. She was dazed and confused and didn't realize she'd been shot until the pain hit her a few minutes later. She believed it was one of the most excruciating pains she'd ever experienced in her life as she yelled out to Cameron that she'd been hit. Cameron immediately went to her side, applied pressure on the wound, and started yelling for a medic.

It took several minutes, but a medic went to her side and started administering first aid. He quickly gave her a pain shot and covered the wound with thick bandages in the front where the bullet entered and, in the back, where it exited. He told her she was lucky because it didn't hit any bones or any large significant arteries. Cameron quickly took her back to where the Captain was directing his troops. Once there, she continued to get care from the medics as they gave her medication and stitched up the wound.

It wasn't long, and all the fighting stopped, and the Captain's soldiers reported everything was under control. The enemy had been killed except for a few that were captured. The Captain told the Air Force commanders about the results of the air mission. He wanted them to know the bombings were successful and several hundred enemies were killed.

The Captain's soldiers began to interrogate the captured soldiers. After several hours of questioning, they found out that the group of soldiers they had killed were the ones that had been in Fresno. When the conditions began worsening in Fresno, they decided to move to a safer location in the foothills, and that's how they ended up in Kettleman City. The soldiers said they had to move from Fresno because the ice got too slushy and soft, and they began losing soldiers who had fallen through the ice and into the water below. They could pull a few of them out alive, but some disappeared under the ice, and they never saw them again. About 100 soldiers that made it into the Sierra Nevada mountains were stuck and couldn't return to base in Fresno.

When the Captain heard about the 100 Russian soldiers in the Sierra Nevada mountains, he contacted General Thompson to let him know. He told him they couldn't cross the valley to get to them, so the General would have to send troops in from the east to intercept them. He'd already informed General Thompson about destroying the headquarters in Kettleman City.

When Cameron found out that the soldiers killed in Kettleman City were some of the soldiers from Fresno, he felt as though he and Staci had accomplished what he wanted to do, and that was to get the soldiers that had killed Brian. Staci was semi-knocked out from the pain medication as Cameron gave her the news about the soldiers.

Cameron and Staci stayed several days with the American soldiers as Staci began her rehabilitation with her left arm in a sling. She got a little stronger every day, so on the 6th day, they talked to the Captain about their desire to go back to meet up with their friends in Pismo Beach. Cameron told the Captain that it looked like he had things under control and no longer needed their help. The captain told them he could always use their support but understood their wanting to return and meet up with their friends. He thanked them for all their help and told them he would give them one of the Russian ATVs full of gas to take with them when they left. They thanked him and told him they would go early the following day. Cameron gave him a salute and told him good luck with his mission and his soldiers. He told the Captain that America depended on him and our military to return America.

Once they decided to return to Pismo Beach, they were anxious to get there. They had backpacks with food, heavy sleeping bags, a shovel, a rope, and a small tent packed on the ATV. They had enough food, so they didn't have to search for any during their journey back. For the next few nights, they found mounds in the ice and set up their small two-person tent behind the mounds to stay hidden and safe from enemy soldiers who might still be out there looking for survivors. Staci's shoulder was still sore, but it improved daily. For the first time after the storm, they were all alone and feeling alright about it.

The following day, they were heading south/east, and whenever they got within a few miles east of the town of Atascadero in the rolling hills area, they heard someone screaming. It seemed distant initially, but the screams began getting louder as they kept going forward. They wanted to know what was happening, so they pulled over the ATV and stopped. Cameron took his weapon off his shoulder and approached the sound, ready to fight if it was a trap.

Cameron whispered to Staci, "I wonder what's going on. That person sounds like they're in pain. I hope the Russians aren't skinning another person alive."

Staci replied, "It doesn't sound like that pain to me. It sounds more like a lonely and frustrating type of pain."

They spread out about twenty feet apart and made their way toward the screams. When they got closer, they could tell someone had fallen into one of the deep ice holes and couldn't escape. Cameron went over to the hole's edge and carefully aimed his rifle down in the hole. There was a young girl in her early teens, and she'd fallen about twenty feet to the bottom. It looked as though she'd been there a few days because it looked as though she'd been trying to claw her way back to the top. It appeared the ice had kept crumbling around her, and there was no way she could get out without someone helping her.

Cameron told Staci to watch around the surrounding area to see if this was a trap when he yelled down at the girl.

"Hey, what are you doing down there in that hole?

The girl immediately retracted into a defensive fetal position, sitting up with her arms wrapped around her legs and pulled toward her body. She slowly said, "I heard your vehicle, so I started screaming. Are you a Russian soldier here to kill me?"

Cameron said, "If I were, you'd already been dead. We're Americans and not here to kill you, but it's a good thing we found you instead of them."

He then had Staci come over and look down and say hello while he went to get the rope from the ATV. Staci introduced herself and asked her how she got down in that hole. She tearfully told her the story about how two Russian soldiers had killed her parents while she was hiding and watching from a hiding place in the house. She told her she'd done what her parents told her to do if the Russians showed up. She had put on heavy-after ski boots and a thick coat, and when the Russians were preoccupied with killing her parents, she left her hiding place and took off running wildly in the dark. She didn't know how far she'd run or where she was going; she just wanted to get away from them before they killed her, too.

She said that's when I fell in here and couldn't get out.

Staci asked her if she was hurt and how long she'd been down there.

She said she'd sprained her left ankle, but it wasn't too bad now. She told her she'd been down there about three days but had lost track of time.

She said, "I have a lot of warm clothes and warm boots on, but it's been cold down here, and I'm freezing and hungry. Can you guys please get me out?"

She wasn't a huge girl and weighed about eighty pounds, so Cameron thought he could pull her out without much trouble. He told her to hold on and that he would try to pull her up. He tied the rope around his waist and threw the other end into the hole. He told her she had to hang on and not let go until he pulled her out. He told her to try and use her feet against the ice wall as he tried to pull her up. Once he had her out of the hole, she was elated, and she immediately hugged Staci and then hugged Cameron. She kept saying thank you to them while she and Staci continued to talk. Cameron rolled up the rope and put it back on the ATV. Staci had a bag of chips in her backpack, so she gave them to the girl and quickly gobbled them down.

Cameron said, "Ok, let's find your house, check on your parents, and ensure there aren't any soldiers still there?" She told them she was optimistic her parents were dead because she saw the soldiers kill them. She started getting anxious when they got close to her house. Cameron and Staci had their weapons drawn and ready to fire as Cameron approached the ice opening. He told her and Staci he would go down and check things out.

Once inside, he found that the soldiers were gone, but the girl's parents were lying dead on the floor where the soldiers had killed them, just like the girl had said. When Cameron first told her that her parents were dead, she broke down in sobs, even though she already knew they were. She was almost hysterical as Staci went over, put her arm around her, and told her she was sorry. Cameron went through the house and checked things out to ensure the soldiers weren't still hiding somewhere.

After several minutes of crying, Staci could ask her what her name was and how old she was. In her tearful voice, she said her name was Amy, and she was thirteen years old.

Cameron covered her parents with blankets, returned to her, and said, "I'm sorry about your parents. Those damn Russians, lucky they didn't see you, or they would've killed you too."

While crying, she said, "I don't know what to do now. Everyone in my family is dead. I don't have anyone. It makes me wish they'd killed me too."

Cameron looked over at Staci as he said, "We'll you have us now, and we'll take care and protect you. We're going to Pismo Beach to meet up with our friends, so you can come with us. You'll have to get some clothes and throw them in one of your school backpacks while we wait for you."

They had only gone a few miles north when they heard gunfire not too far away. Cameron told the girls he wanted to check it out and see what happened. He had them stay low as he snuck close enough to look and see. When he was close enough, he saw two soldiers who had a survivor pinned down and were trying to kill him. Cameron had the girls stay back as he carefully aimed and quickly took out the two soldiers.

Once they were sure, the soldiers were dead and didn't have any others with them. Cameron slowly stood up and waved to the survivor. Cameron talked briefly to him, and the man thanked him for the help. After the encounter, they then continued their way to Pismo. They heard sporadic gunfire on their way back but avoided any more confrontations with soldiers.

When they first got to the Hotel, Thomas, Kirstin, and Jason came running out to welcome them back. They wanted to know what happened to Staci's arm but were happy to see each other. They were also anxious to hear about what had happened since they had last seen each other.

Staci quickly introduced them to Amy and told them her parents had been killed in Atascadero by the soldiers, but she had escaped. She said to them that Amy was going to stay with them.

Kirstin went over, put her arm around Amy's shoulder, and said, "Yes, we're glad to have you stay with us."

Cameron pulled Thomas and Jason aside and said, "We got the Russian soldiers from Fresno that killed Brian. They had moved their headquarters to Kettleman City because the water in the valley ran them out. They're all dead now except for about 100 of them that went into the mountains looking for survivors. You were right, Jason; it was a good thing we didn't go back to the Cabin; we'd be fighting them for our survival right now. We told the General about them, and he will send troops to get them from the east."

Captain Singletary's people are doing their part to wipe out the Russian Soldiers. It looks like the military is getting control of things, and it won't be long before all the Russian soldiers are gone. Thomas smiled as they hugged each other and said, "Thank God. We're glad you are back. We missed you guys."

The group had a meeting later that night and talked about where they felt safe until all the Russians' fighting was over. Cameron said, "I don't think things in America will be the same for a long time. It will take a while for all the ice to melt completely and for the water to recede. If we stay here, we won't have to deal with the flooding all over America. Eventually, the dams and everything will be repaired, but it might take several years. It may take a long time before we can return to the San Joaquin Valley or any place else in California. Pismo Beach might be our permanent home and the best place for us to be."

***

***

Chapter 19

Not being a man to sit back and take a beating without lashing back at his enemies, the United States president decided to retaliate against Russia for the failed attempt of their massive take-over of the United States. Because of his anger and frustration with Russia, the President decided he would implement the HAARP Earthquake Weather Warfare Program that America also possessed against Russia.

At the direction of the President of the United States, the military was able to infiltrate a team of Special Forces into Russia. They carried with them ground-penetrating radar equipment used in creating earthquakes. Once inside Russia, they split up into two teams and maneuvered into strategic places to cause two massive earthquakes across Russia. After they were in position, the Special Forces soldiers placed the equipment above substantial fault lines in some of Russia's major cities.

They could use ground-penetrating radar to beam pulses of polarized high-frequency radio waves deep into the ionosphere (known as Elf Waves). The vibrations are finely tuned and adjusted so the bounced-ground penetrating beam can target a particular area for a specific time. The equipment could beam massive energy beams into the ground for an extended period and cause significant earthquakes. Once they're placed in position, the electromagnetic waves can cause an earthquake anywhere around the world artificially through electromagnetic waves. *

On the President's command, the electromagnetic waves were unleashed in Russia's designated locations for an extended period. It caused massive and devastating 10.0 earthquakes. After the first few quakes, they waited thirty minutes and hit them with another massive dose of electromagnetic waves, causing another vast 10.0 quake. Hundreds of smaller aftershocks and tremors followed the gigantic earthquakes, and the quakes caused widespread infrastructural damage.

Gas lines exploded into giant fireballs, and incredible explosions were seen and felt all over Russia. It looked as though a nuclear bomb had been unleashed on Russia, and most of the significant buildings were destroyed in and around Moscow and other major cities. Most of the significant buildings were reduced to nothing more than piles of rubble, and millions of Russian people were killed in the quakes.

Once the outcome of the earthquakes in Russia was known to the President of the United States, he felt somewhat vindicated for what Russia tried to do to America. When the President of the United States was finally able to talk with the president of Russia, there was extreme anger and bitterness on both sides for the loss of lives and the destruction of the infrastructure of both countries. Russia and the United States suffered significant losses in the Weather Warfare System. Both countries had previously touted it as merely an experimental and a non-functional program. Both Presidents agreed to a cease-fire and promised not to use nuclear weapons against each other. However, neither side would admit defeat through all the deaths and devastation.

Acknowledgments

I want to give a special thanks to Rita Toews for developing the book's cover for me. Rita Toews of www.yourebookcover.com[1]

Credit for cover photo: href="[https://www.canstockphoto.com"https://www.canstockphoto.com' Can Stock Photo / zabelin</a>

* Wikipedia, the free encyclopedia – High-Frequency Research Program

I want to give a huge thanks to my sister, Sharon Duvall, for editing the book. I am grateful for her help.

---

1. https://eur03.safelinks.protection.outlook.com/?url=http%3A%2F%2Fwww.yourebookcover.com&data=02%7C01%7C%7Cd46d0a8b76754dcf753908d721f5cd8e%7C84df9e7fe9f640afb435aaaaaaaaaaaa%7C1%7C0%7C6370152121110091565&sdata=4ZIC4WlIJKwegJ%2B1ha7SoPzcH6%2Bt%2BSwI%2BXqdzyg8HJ4%3D&reserved=0

Other books by this author

Twenty-One Months
    From the Darkness of My Mind
    Unearthly Realms
    American Terrorist – A Grandfather's Revenge
    American Terrorist – The Revenge Continues
    American Terrorist – The Silent Killer
    Night Crawlers
    Night Crawlers – Reign of Terror
    Night Crawlers – The Nightmares Continue
    In Defense of Mankind
    Zak Thomas – The Monster Hunter
    Lost Waters
    Love me now, Don't wait - Poetry